Still More
SCARY
STORIES
for Sleep-Overs

By Q. L. Pearce

Illustrated by Dwight Been

Lowell House
Juvenile
Los Angeles

5 7 9 11 12 10 8 6
ISBN: 1-56565-202-9

Typeset by Carolyn Wendt from a design by Michele Lanci-Altomare

———◆———

———◆———

Contents

1. Night of the Kii-Kwan . . . 7

2. A Special Pair . . . 17

3. The Gunslinger . . . 29

4. The Slime Mutants of Clear Lake . . . 39

5. The Storm . . . 51

6. Homecoming . . . 63

7. Portrait of Evil . . . 71

8. All the Time in the World . . . 85

9. Household Help . . . 97

10. The Snow Cave . . . 107

11. The Fabulous Flyers . . . 119

Night of the Kii-Kwan

he moment he saw the package wrapped in brown paper on the dining-room table, Matthew knew where it was from. First of all, it was a Friday, and the packages always arrived on Fridays. They were always wrapped with coarse, strong twine, too. He set his schoolbooks on the table and lifted the heavy box. His name was neatly lettered in his mother's clear handwriting.

"So you've found it."

Matthew looked up. His grandmother was standing in the kitchen doorway, smiling.

"Yes, Gran," he said. "It feels like there's a lot of stuff in this one. I can't wait to get a look at what's inside."

Matthew was very proud of his mother. She was a scientist, an anthropologist, who studied the traditions of Native American peoples. For the past three years his mom had spent several weeks each spring in the mountains near the site of an ancient village studying the history of a small, mysterious tribe of Choklow people. Twice a month, she would send home a package of notes and objects that local people had given her to help with her work.

Matthew wanted to be an anthropologist, too, when he grew up. Each year when she came home, his mother had allowed Matthew to help her as she organized the material that she had collected on her trip. This year he was entrusted with the job of opening each package and checking to see that everything had arrived in order.

"Well, aren't you going to open it?" Gran asked.

Matthew tugged the twine away, tore through the paper and opened the box. Inside there was a flat stone for grinding grain, a beaded necklace decorated with feathers, and a pipe carved from a single piece of grayish wood.

Everything had been labeled, and Matthew checked each item against a list his mother had enclosed. But he was more interested in two spiral notebooks in the bottom of the box. These contained his mother's notes. She had been collecting stories from the descendant of a tribal medicine man, and some of them were pretty scary.

Matthew sat down and opened the first book. It was mostly about the kinds of dwellings the Choklow had built when they first settled in the mountains. When he opened the second notebook, he let out a low whistle. Tucked into the front was a colored-pencil drawing of a strange-looking creature. The body, tall and muscular, looked human, almost normal . . . except that it had very long fingers and toes tipped with savage-looking, curved claws. But the head sent a chill right through him. It was large and wolfish. Double rows of long, pointed teeth lined the open jaws. At the front, a pair of daggerlike fangs overlapped the lower jaw. Black fur covered the creature's head and neck and ended like a shaggy collar over its shoulders.

It was the eyes, though, that really caught Matthew's attention. They were wide and fiery red, with a thin slit of black at the centers. He looked at the drawing from different angles, but the eyes always seemed to be looking right at him.

The first page in the notebook explained that the beast was a type of legendary creature called the Kii-Kwan. Matthew read on about the legend of the creature. "Cool," he said under his breath when he had finished reading. "This will be perfect for tonight."

His grandmother had returned to the kitchen. Matthew checked to see that she was out of hearing range, then he picked up the telephone and punched in a number. After a couple of rings his friend, Joey, answered.

"Joey, I got a package today," Matthew said softly.

"Matt? Is that you? How come you're whispering? I can hardly hear you."

Matthew raised his voice a little. "I can't talk any louder. My grandmother is in the kitchen. I got a package, and it's got a good story in it. Looks really creepy. You want to call the guys and tell them we're going to meet at the clearing?"

Joey sounded hesitant. "I don't know, Matt. I almost got caught sneaking back in last time."

"Oh, come on—sneaking out is part of the fun!" goaded Matthew. "The legend is about wolf people that devour their victims and chomp their bones into tiny bits."

The line was silent for another moment, then Joey croaked, "Wolf people?"

"With red eyes and long, sharp claws," Matthew coaxed.

"Okay. Count me in," Joey said. "I'll call the rest of the guys and see you at midnight."

• • • • • • • • • •

At 11:30 that night, Matthew left his room, tiptoed past his snoring grandmother and slipped out the front door. He ran to the end of his block and then turned uphill, into the woods. He had a small flashlight with him, but he really didn't need it. The moon was full and he could have found his way to the clearing blindfolded.

Matthew and his friends Joey, Linc, Ron and Zack had formed the Terror Society a year ago. At least once a month they met at the clearing to tell scary stories. They had even tried to hold séances a couple of times to conjure up spirits of the dead. At first Matt hadn't been very good at storytelling, because he had had a hard time making things up, but then he started telling the tales of the medicine man that he read in his mom's notes. Everyone got really scared. Now they met whenever a package arrived that contained a new tale of fright.

As he neared the meeting place, Matthew could see a glimmer of light through the trees. He stepped into the clearing and saw that the others were already hunched around a small fire. Smiling to himself, Matthew decided to really set the stage for his story.

"That's right," he said aloud. He was pleased that the other boys jumped when he spoke. "Stay as close to the fire as you can, because it is the only thing that *they* fear. It is the only thing that can protect you from them."

"Fr . . . fr . . . from who?" Zack faked being frightened. He was already into it.

Matthew slowly approached the fire and stretched out his hands to warm them. He looked into the eyes of each boy one at a time, then spoke in a hushed tone. "The Kii-Kwan. They roam these very woods, hungry and thirsty, looking for a meal of tender human flesh and thirst-quenching blood. With the cunning of an animal and the cruelty of a human, they stalk helpless victims and tear them to shreds, even cracking open their bones to reach the marrow inside."

His audience was hooked. Matthew continued on with the legend, adding a few frightening details of his own. When he had finished, he paused for effect, then pulled his mother's drawing from his jacket. "Behold!—the face of the Kii-Kwan!" It was a little dramatic, but it worked. Everyone gasped. In the firelight, the red eyes of the beast seemed to glitter. Then all of the boys broke out in nervous laughter.

They took turns looking at the frightful drawing. Zack shivered. "I'm not so sure I want to cut back through the woods if these guys are out there."

"Don't worry," Matthew assured him. "They only hunt at night under the cover of fog. And as you can see," he said, gesturing toward the full moon, "this doesn't seem to be their kind of night."

Even so, the boys all walked back through the woods together and didn't split up until they were near their homes.

· · · · · · · · · ·

Two weeks later, another package arrived. Matthew was disappointed that there were no more stories, but he did find another notebook. The handwriting was tiny and irregular, nothing like his mother's, and the pages were filled with what seemed to be instructions. Some of the words were odd sounding, but he did recognize a name . . . *Kii-Kwan*. It was repeated several times. Matthew read over the scrawled instructions a couple of times, then suddenly realized what it was. It was a spell to conjure up the Kii-Kwan! The whole book was filled with spells.

This time, Matthew had no trouble at all convincing Joey to slip out. He simpy told him that he had something better than a scary story. He had a notebook full of magic spells.

That night Matthew was so excited and anxious to try one of the spells that he was the first to arrive at the clearing. He took some time to gather up a pile of dry wood and started a fire. One by one, the others arrived.

Linc had brought along some face paint. "I thought it would help the ritual," he explained, smearing a bold blue stripe on his cheek.

The boys laughed and kidded each other as they painted their faces with lines and dots of color. Finally, Joey stood in front of the flickering fire and called the group to order.

"It's time," he said slowly. "The preparations are complete. We must choose a spell."

The other boys snickered, but then they played along and set their faces in somber expressions. Then Ron turned to Matthew. "What are our choices?"

"As far as I can tell," Matthew answered, "the easiest ones are bringing rain and finding an underground spring."

Zack laughed out loud. "Oh, great. Don't you have anything for finding treasure or something?"

"Nope," Matthew said, still flipping through the notebook. "That's it. The others look kind of dangerous."

"Then it's rain," Linc suggested. "That'll be more fun than having to dig a well!"

The boys agreed and began to follow the instructions in the notebook word for word. They chanted the spell together and moved around the fire in a kind of clumsy dance until Joey stopped them.

"Quiet!" he demanded.

They all stood perfectly still.

"Did you hear that? It sounded like thunder."

"You're hearing things," Linc laughed and elbowed his friend. "Look," he said, pointing up. "There isn't a cloud in the sky. Besides, I'm tired of this. What else is in the book? Isn't there anything scary?"

Matthew looked from one boy to the next. He didn't want to disappoint his friends. "Well, there is one thing. But it sounds too scary to me."

"What is it?" Ron asked.

Matthew bit his lower lip and hesitated. He wasn't really

sure anymore that he wanted to do this. What if it worked? "Well," he said quietly, "there is a spell to call the Kii-Kwan."

At first no one spoke. Then Joey broke the silence. "You mean those wolf monsters? Why would we want to bring them around here?"

Suddenly Linc laughed. "Oh, come on, you guys. This stuff doesn't really work. It's just a goof. It's for fun. Let's do the spell!"

Joey wasn't convinced. "What if this stuff *does* work?"

Linc looked at his friend. "We've been doing a rain dance for 15 minutes. Are you wet?"

Everyone laughed. Linc was right. "Let's do it!" they shouted. Then they huddled around the fire and carefully recited each part of the spell for the Kii-Kwan. Nothing happened.

"Maybe we ought to dance around for this one, too," Ron joked and whirled around. As the other boys laughed he whirled faster, then tripped and tumbled toward the fire. He fell heavily.

"Are you okay?" Matthew asked.

"Yeah," Ron sat up. He held his hand out toward the fire. "I think I might have cut my hand on that piece of wood, though." A drop of blood formed on the side of Ron's hand and dripped onto one of the heated rocks that ringed the fire pit. As it hit, the blood spattered and sizzled. A tiny puff of steam rose from the rock and swirled toward the woods. As the boys watched, the puff expanded and developed into a dense fog.

"What's going on?" Joey sounded frightened.

"I don't know," Matthew said. "Maybe we should go."

But before they could take a step, there was a rustling sound in the woods. The boys backed up toward the fire. In the deepening fog they could see dozens of pairs of glowing red eyes.

"It's them!" Ron moaned in terror. "It's the Kii-Kwan. We've brought them here!"

A deep, vicious snarl rose from the shadows.

"What are we going to do?" Joey was almost in tears. "Does it say anything about how to make them go away?"

Matthew flipped through the book. "I don't see anything," he said, beginning to panic. Then suddenly he remembered something. "But the first legend said that they won't come near fire. We have to keep the fire going! There's plenty of wood. If we can keep the fire going until sunrise, we can hold them off!"

"That's right!" Joey sounded hopeful. "I remember you said something about that. All we have to do is—" He suddenly stopped. "Listen," he whispered.

"Oh, no," Linc groaned. "It worked. That stupid rain dance . . . it worked."

The thunder rolled again, and as the first drops of rain splattered down, the fire sputtered, dimmed and left them alone in the thickening fog.

A Special Pair

he's gonna love this!" Alex said excitedly as he and his dad set up the hamster habitat, complete with a large, bright-yellow exercise wheel. Alex opened the box from the pet store and scooped up two identical hamsters with reddish gold and snowy white fur. The gifts that Alex and Amy exchanged on their shared birthday were always in pairs. It was their own special way to celebrate being twins.

"This," Alex said with certainty, "is the best idea I've come up with yet!" He covered the habitat with a sheet of red wrapping paper and punched small holes in the top to provide plenty of air for the little animals. Then his dad helped him to place the gift on a table in the family room.

The children had a hard time being patient during dinner. Alex was very curious about the package that Amy had brought home with her. Finally, after the table had been cleared, it was time to open the gifts. Amy opened her present first.

"Oh, Alex," she squealed as she looked at the furry creatures. "They're adorable!" She picked up both of her fluffy pets at once and looked them in the eyes. "I will call you Castor and Pollux," she informed the wriggling animals, "after the twins we read about in Greek mythology."

Alex rolled his eyes, and Amy rolled hers right back. "Just open your present," she said.

Alex ripped open his gift. His eyes sparkled as he read the label on the box. "Walkie-talkies! Thanks!"

"They run on batteries," Amy pointed out. "We can use them anywhere."

Within a week, Amy had taught both hamsters to come to her when she made a special whistling sound, and Alex had become an expert with the walkie-talkies. At night the twins kept the walkie-talkie units in their bedrooms and whispered jokes and secrets until they fell asleep. They were grateful to have them when Mrs. Bragg left and the new baby-sitter arrived.

"Why isn't Mrs. Bragg going to stay with us?" Amy asked, watching her mother snap her suitcase shut.

"Mrs. Bragg has a new grandson. She has gone to stay with her daughter and help out for a few weeks. But this sitter is highly recommended. I've already had a nice, long talk with her, and I'm sure you will like her."

"I'm sure we will," Amy said, trying to convince herself. "Besides, you and Dad will only be gone for the weekend."

But Amy wasn't quite as sure of herself when the new sitter finally arrived. The woman's name was Clara. Crouched at the top of the stairs, Amy and Alex watched as Clara marched into the house. The twins looked at each other, and without a word, they decided they didn't like her.

"Alex! Amy!" their mom called. "Come here, please."

Slowly, they made their way down the stairs. They stood looking up at the intruder. "This is Clara," their mother said. "She will stay with you while we are gone. Now, be good kids and do as she says. I'm counting on you."

Clara looked from one twin to the other. She seemed very pleased. "Oh, I'm sure we'll get along just fine, Mrs. Rogers. You have no idea how glad I am to meet this special pair." Her eyes glittered so wickedly that Alex gasped. He looked at his mother to see whether she had noticed it, too. But she was already double-checking her list to be sure she hadn't forgotten anything.

A moment later, after hugs and a last-minute search for the camera, their parents were gone. Amy and Alex were alone with Clara, who smiled crookedly and raised one eyebrow. "Now, why don't we get to know one another a little better? Let's sit down, and you can tell me all about yourselves."

• • • • • • • • • •

Before bedtime the twins watched their favorite television show, but Clara paid little attention to the screen. She stared boldly at the children. Alex, trying to be nice, offered her some of the buttery popcorn he had made.

"No," she said, waving it away. "I'm on a special diet. But you two go ahead and fill up. There's nothing sweeter than a pair of plump youngsters."

Alex glanced sideways at Amy. His expression said, "Is she weird or what?" He placed the bowl back on the table without watching what he was doing.

"Look out!" Amy cried. But it was too late. The bowl clanked against her half-empty soda glass and toppled it to the floor. The glass cracked into several large pieces.

Alex leaned over to pick it up, then pulled back his hand. "Ouch! I cut my finger!"

Clara grabbed at his hand. Her eyes were fiery. "Is it bleeding? Let me see!"

"It's okay," Alex said. He tried to pull his hand away, but Clara held on tightly. With a paper napkin, she dabbed at the tiny cut.

Alex squirmed in her grasp. "Let me go!"

The sitter seemed to gain control of herself. "I'm sorry. I just didn't expect such a . . . " The excited expression on her face rearranged itself into something resembling concern. " . . . such an unfortunate accident. Perhaps it is time that you two went up to bed. I'll clean up this mess. Then I'm going to take my evening walk. Don't worry, I'll be back before you know it."

"She's so creepy," Amy whispered to Alex as the twins slowly climbed the stairs. "I think she's up to something."

"That's silly," Alex said. But as he glanced back, he saw Clara slip the bloodstained napkin into her pocket.

Alex didn't know how long he had been asleep when he heard his sister's frightened voice. *"Alex! Can you hear me?"*

"Amy?" He picked up his walkie-talkie unit. "What's wrong?"

"She's right outside the door. What should I do?"

Alex thought quickly. "Don't let her know you're awake. Just see what happens. If she tries to hurt you, I'll stop her." Through the walkie-talkie, he heard Amy's shallow breathing as her bedroom door creaked open. He slipped out of bed and tiptoed across the room. Gripping the handle of his baseball bat, he opened his door just a crack and scanned the darkened hallway. A shadow stepped from Amy's room, and then Alex heard footsteps retreating down the stairs. He rushed into his sister's room.

"Amy! Are you all right?"

"Yes. But it's so odd. She took my hairbrush! What do you suppose she wants with it?"

Alex tapped one finger against his lips. He thought about the bloodstained napkin . . . and now this. It sounded like voodoo or something. But that was crazy.

"Look," he finally whispered. "I think I should search her room. We'll wait until tomorrow, then you make up some excuse to get her away from the house."

"I don't know if that's such a good idea," Amy said.

"Do you have a better one?"

The following morning, Alex was shaken awake. Amy was leaning over him. "Castor and Pollux are gone!" she said. "I've looked for them everywhere, but I can't find them!"

Alex tried to calm his sister. "They're probably somewhere in the house. I'll help you look."

Amy turned to leave. "Wait!" Alex exclaimed. "That's it! You ask Clara to help you look for Castor and Pollux outside while I look in the house. That will give me a chance to see if anything is suspicious in her room."

"Okay," Amy agreed. "I'll ask her right now."

Alex dressed and hurried downstairs in time to see Amy and Clara go out to the backyard. He went straight to Clara's room and quietly opened the door.

At first nothing caught his attention . . . but then his gaze fell on a tuft of reddish gold and white fur on the floor. He picked it up and examined it.

"Hamster fur?" Alex made the special whistling sound that Amy had taught the hamsters to respond to. Something chattered from within the closet and Alex moved toward the sound. Slowly, he reached for the knob. His fingers had just touched it when the door to the bedroom flew open. Alex whirled and came face to face with Clara.

"What are you doing in here?" she demanded.

"I . . . well, I . . . I was looking for Castor and Pollux, Amy's hamsters. I thought I heard them." He cringed as Clara leaned in close to him.

"They're not here," she said.

"But I'm sure I heard . . . "

"They're not here," she said firmly.

Alex glanced at the closet door. "I must have made a

mistake," he lied. He left quickly and went to his room. Moments later, Amy knocked at the door and slipped in.

"Did you find anything?" she asked.

"No!" Alex said sourly. "You were supposed to keep her outside for a while and give me some time."

Amy looked at him strangely. "I did, Alex. Clara has been outside with me all of this time."

"Oh, right! Then why did she walk in while I was in her room and scare me to death?"

Amy took her brother's arm and steered him to the window. "Alex, Clara has been outside with me—she's still out there!"

Alex looked down to see Clara searching among the bushes in the yard. "Then who . . . how did she . . . ? I don't know what's going on here, but if she is up to something, she's going to have to make her move tonight. Mom and Dad will be home tomorrow. I think the answer is in her closet. She sure didn't want me to look in there. Tonight, we'll have to figure out a way to see what she's hiding."

• • • • • • • • • •

All day long the twins kept a close eye on Clara. Finally, after dinner, Clara announced that she was going to take her evening walk. The twins watched her leave.

Alex rushed to the door and locked it. "There—now she won't be able to sneak in on us!" Smiling, he held up a key that glittered in the light from the hall. "I took this from her coat pocket this afternoon. Now, come on. This may be our only chance to find out what she's up to."

The children made their way to the guest room at the back of the house. A dull, reddish light shone on the carpet at the base of the slightly open door. Alex and Amy crept as close as they dared and peered into Clara's room. Bathed in a faint red glow, it appeared to be empty. Alex stepped into the room and halted. Two children, a boy and a girl, stood gazing out of the open window. Each had wide bands strapped to their wrists. The bands were attached by tubes to some sort of machine with gauges. A thick fluid was pulsing through the tubes and into needles stuck into each child's wrist. The machine was the source of the crimson glow.

Slowly, ever so slowly, the youngsters turned. Alex felt his jaw drop. It was like looking into a mirror. He was standing face to face with exact likenesses of Amy and himself. "What is happening?"

"What is happening?" his image repeated. It was like listening to his own voice.

Alex felt dizzy. "This is impossible."

"This is impossible," repeated his double.

"Not really," said a voice behind him. Alex reeled around to lock into Clara's gaze. She had Amy by the shoulder. "It was quite simple, in fact. It only took a few moments for the duplicator to produce the shells. All I needed was something to animate them . . . a sample of hair . . . a little blood . . . a couple of . . . well, let's call them volunteers." She held up a handful of gold and white fur. It was stained with dried blood.

"Castor and Pollux," Amy moaned.

"Yes, you were quite right, Alex. You did hear them this

morning, but I couldn't very well let you open the closet door and see them halfway through their transition. But now it is almost complete, and they will soon take your places quite nicely. Even your parents won't know the difference. No one will ever suspect that you are missing. Other parents will continue to hire me to baby-sit, and I can go on with my captures without interruption. Now, are you ready to go?"

"Not with you!" With some reserve of strength, Alex charged across the room and knocked Clara off her balance. He grabbed his sister's hand. "Let's get out of here!" Together they raced to the front door. Alex fumbled for a moment with the lock, then yanked it open, but . . .

Outside, Clara loomed above them in the doorway. Behind her was what looked like a bizarre craft of some sort. Its edges were vague, and it was bathed in the same reddish glow they had seen in Clara's room.

"You might as well come along quietly," Clara said. "It really won't be so bad. We have a nice habitat all prepared for you. I think you will like the exercise wheel. It will keep you occupied until you reach your final destination."

Alex felt his will seeping away, "Who are you? Where are you taking us?"

"We are the hunters," Clara answered simply. "We come from out there." She gestured toward the constellation Gemini. "Don't worry, we already have plenty more of your kind to keep you company for the trip. In fact, there are hundreds of our clever 'replacements' already in position. You tasty little morsels will not be missed." She grinned widely, exposing a mouth full of daggerlike teeth.

Alex watched as the door to the craft yawned silently open. "There are more of you?" he asked. "Is that how you could be in the garden with Amy and in your room at the same time?"

"Oh, no. That was a simple projection in the garden, an illusion. There are, indeed, more of us—dozens, in fact—but I am quite special, you see." Clara beamed with pride as she nudged Amy and Alex along. "I only hunt *pairs*. Now hurry along. We don't want you to be late for dinner!"

⟹◇⟸

The Gunslinger

omstock City was one of the most famous frontier towns of the American West, and Chris prided himself on knowing all of the details of its incredible history. Chris and his buddies Michael and Eddie often took a shortcut through the old cemetery on the way home from Comstock Middle School, and Chris would tell his friends the legends of the men and women who rested beneath the worn tombstones. Like everyone else in town, Michael and Eddie were already familiar with most of the stories, but Chris had become a real expert. His favorite tales were of the outlaws—brutal gunslingers who had terrorized the town a century before. One very fierce gang had been feared throughout the territory. Their leader, D. B. Rance, had had a particularly evil career. Rance had killed seven men by the time he was eighteen.

"He's the meanest of anybody here in this cemetery," Chris assured his friends. The boys had stopped at the side of Rance's grave. "He even killed men who had dropped to their knees begging for their lives." Chris saw that this made an impression on the other boys. "But he was a coward, too. He was known for shooting people in the back."

Michael studied the grave. "Wasn't he killed in a shoot-out?"

Chris loved the attention of his friends, and he played it up for all that it was worth. He tucked his thumbs in his belt loops and placed one foot against the tombstone. "Yeah. He was gunned down . . . him and his whole gang. Rance was the first one to go. He got a bullet right between the eyes and dropped where he stood. But they're all here." Chris made a sweeping gesture with his hand toward the back of the cemetery grounds.

Eddie shivered. "Hey, you guys. It's starting to get late. We don't want to be here after dark."

Chris smirked. "Why not? You're not afraid of anything in here, are you?"

"C'mon, Chris." Michael picked his bike up from the ground where he had left it. "Eddie's right."

"I don't believe you guys!" Chris laughed. "These jerks are dead. *I'm* not afraid of them. I wouldn't even have been afraid of them when they were alive." He made his point by kicking at Rance's aged gravestone.

"You'd better not do that, Chris," Eddie warned.

Chris cocked his head. "Why not? I really don't believe you guys. You're chicken . . . afraid of a dead man!"

"You wouldn't say that if he were standing right in front of you," Eddie shot back.

"Sure I would," said Chris. "If I'd have lived here a hundred years ago, I would have been even meaner than D. B. Rance. I would have joined his gang. No, I probably would have been the *leader* of his gang!" Excitedly, Chris turned to face the grave. "Do you hear that, D. B. Rance? I'm not afraid of you. If you're so tough, I challenge you to a battle right here and now!"

Chris stood defiantly, his fists clenched. He had always secretly wished that he could have lived in the days of the Old West. He thought it would have been great to have marched down the center of a dusty street while the townspeople fled for cover . . . to have faced down an opponent and waited for the right second to draw his gun.

The boys stood, barely breathing. The only sound was the creaking of the leafless branches of a huge dead tree beside the grave. Finally, Chris laughed. "You see?" He felt a thrill, as though he'd actually won a battle. "I told you. Rance is a coward."

"Like you said . . . he's dead," Michael muttered.

Chris laughed again. "If he was everything that some people around here say he was, even *that* wouldn't stop him. He's a coward and a phony!" To make his point, Chris kicked at the gravestone again. But since it had been raining a lot lately and the ground was soft, this time the thin stone quivered slightly, and a small chunk fell off the top and landed with a sickening thud.

Just then, the wind picked up unexpectedly and the tree branches overhead swayed and groaned. Chris was startled. To cover his sudden fear, he bent down and picked up the small, ragged-edged piece of stone. It felt cold and heavy in his hand. "I'll just keep this as a souvenir."

"Maybe you'd better not take it, Chris," Eddie advised nervously. "Maybe you should just put it back."

Chris slipped the stone into his backpack and swaggered over to his bike. "Who's going to make me?" He tilted his head toward the grave. "Him?"

· · · · · · · · · ·

Once they were away from the cemetery, Michael and Eddie quickly got over their fear. By the time the boys reached their block, they were all laughing about how Chris had bested that two-bit gunslinger.

"I guess he couldn't have been all that tough," Michael admitted. "Or he wouldn't have gotten caught in an ambush."

"Yeah, I'd never let anybody sneak up on *me*," Chris boasted as he opened the front gate to his yard. As he stepped inside and pulled the gate closed, he caught sight of something in the soft dirt beside the path. It was a fresh print, a big one . . . a *boot* print. Chris stared at the print for a moment, trying to decide who might have made it. Then he realized that his friends were already pedaling off down the street. "See you tomorrow," he yelled after them.

After dinner he told his mom he had lots of homework and headed upstairs to his room to read the newest issue of his favorite comic book, *Spook Mansion*. He flopped down on his bed and had barely started the first story, about a boy trapped in a haunted fun park, when his mom called out.

"Chris!"

He pretended not to hear her.

"Chris!" she called a little louder. "I know you can hear me. You promised to take out the trash right after dinner."

He sighed but still didn't answer.

"CHRIS!"

"All right! I'll be there in a minute," he called.

"Not in a minute—right *now*, young man."

Chris could tell by the tone of his mother's voice that it would be a good idea to do as she asked. Grumbling, he tossed the comic aside and stomped half-heartedly downstairs. His mother was waiting for him.

"And when you're finished, you can get your homework and do it down here on the table instead of barricading yourself in your room to read comic books," she said firmly.

"I wasn't reading comic books," Chris lied, wondering how she always knew. He pulled on his jacket and grabbed the plastic bag sitting beside the kitchen table, then shoved open the screen door and let it slam behind him.

Still muttering, he shuffled out into the backyard and to the alley gate. It was always pretty deserted in his neighborhood at night. There was a streetlight just a few feet from the gate, but he still didn't like being alone in the alley. He hurriedly lifted the lid on the metal trash can and threw the bag of garbage inside and slammed the lid back down.

As soon as he turned toward the open gate again, he noticed a tall figure at the darkened end of the alley. His heart began to race, but for some reason Chris couldn't seem to move his feet. The shadow walked very slowly and deliberately toward him. He could hear the dull sound of boot heels hitting the dusty pavement.

Chris lowered his eyes, terrified to look at the approaching figure, but somehow he knew who it was. "Please, don't let it be him," he moaned. But when Chris raised his eyes again, he felt a wave of horror flood over him. He was looking at the cruel face of D. B. Rance.

It was the same evil face that he had seen in old pictures in local tourist guides, but with one difference. Unlike in the pictures, there was a neat, black hole right between the gunslinger's eyes . . . an ugly wound from the bullet that had ended his life a century before.

The phantom stopped a few feet away and locked his cold eyes on Chris. He was dressed in faded clothes and a worn, rotting leather jacket. He pushed his jacket back on one side and Chris could see a shining pistol strapped to his left hip. Rance held his left arm so that his hand was only inches from the gun. His fingers, curled up like claws, were twitching as if he couldn't wait to use the weapon once more.

Chris looked down at his own trembling hands. "A ghost can't hurt me," he said aloud, trying to convince himself. "He isn't real." Chris stole a look at the gate. It was open. He tried with all his might to run, but his terror held him anchored to one spot.

Rance twisted his mouth into a terrible grin and spoke. "What's the matter, boy? You a coward or something? I don't think there's anything I hate worse than a coward. Unless it's a *thief* and a coward."

Chris saw the specter's hand flinch, and he forced himself to move. He made a clumsy, stumbling dive for the gate and landed facedown in the alley. Afraid to look up, he crawled along, trying to escape the gruesome ghost of D. B. Rance.

Suddenly, Chris realized that it wasn't the blacktop of the alley that he was dragging himself across, but dirt. He dug his fingers around handfuls of cold clay. The only sound was the creaking of branches in the wind.

Finally, Chris opened his eyes. He didn't know how it had happened, but he was stretched across the cold earth of the cemetery, and he wasn't alone. As frightened as he was, Chris recognized all the figures standing around him— Rufus Thomas, Hayworth Weiser, Kevin O'Donnell . . . all men who had died that day with D. B. Rance. Even Jack Peyton, the only gang member to have survived the gun battle, stood staring down at him. Chris saw the deep red mark of the rope on the ghost's pale neck.

Slowly, Chris raised himself up to his knees, then to his feet. The phantoms didn't move. Gathering his courage, Chris whirled around and raced toward the cemetery fence. He didn't get far. D. B. Rance stepped from behind the old dead tree and stood directly in his path.

The wind howled, and the dried branches of the tree trembled like long-fingered hands reaching up into the night sky. Chris could hear the ancient wood snapping and crackling. He fell to his knees beside the gravestone that he had kicked over earlier. He remembered Eddie's words: *You wouldn't say that if he were standing right in front of you.*

"I didn't mean any of what I said," Chris sobbed. The gunfighter eased toward him like a predator. The phantom gang looked on silently. Chris could smell dampness and decay as the thing crouched down, put its face right next to his, and touched the barrel of a Colt .45 to Chris's head.

"You took something of mine," Rance growled. Chris cringed at his rancid breath. "*Nobody* steals from me."

Chris peered up into the horrible eyes and backed away just slightly. As he moved he felt the weight of something in his jacket pocket. He slipped his trembling fingers inside, pulled the broken piece of gravestone from his pocket and held it in the palm of his outstretched hand. Slowly, the gunslinger reached out and took it. Chris felt the icy, cold brush of the dead man's hand.

"Please," Chris begged. "You've got what you want. Now let me go." He had to yell above the sound of the wind. Above him the tree branches whipped back and forth as if trying to escape from the ghostly gunslinger, too.

Rance laughed and the others joined him. The hideous noise nearly drowned out the rising moan of the wind and the thrashing of the tree branches. With a savage look on his face, Rance pulled back the hammer of his gun. Chris stiffened. The wail of the wind continued to rise as Rance squeezed the trigger. Chris heard a loud crack.

For a moment everything seemed to spin around him, then it was still again, and Chris became aware that he was still crouching on the ground.

"I'm all right," he mumbled, half stunned. "He can't . . . he really can't hurt me." Without looking back, Chris rose unsteadily to his feet. Willing his legs to move, he made a mad dash for the fence at the edge of the graveyard. But the fence didn't get any closer. No matter how hard he ran, he seemed to be staying in the same place.

In total terror, Chris spun around and saw Rance and the other spirits grinning wickedly. Rance was standing over a lifeless body stretched limply across the gunslinger's grave. In horror, Chris saw that it was his own! One of the massive, rotten branches from the tree above the grave had finally splintered in the wind and fallen, hitting him in the head.

Rance snarled. "Hey, boys! Looks like we have a new member in the gang." He threw back his head in a shriek of horrible laughter, as the wind rose and whipped away both the sounds of the laugh and Chris's screams.

━━▷◆◁━━

The Slime Mutants of Clear Lake

iane pulled on her favorite sweatshirt. It was so faded and worn that the message on the front, "Make Earth Day Every Day," was barely readable. As she was closing her backpack, the door to her room opened and her mom leaned in. "Mr. Carter is outside in the van," she said, smiling. "Are you ready?"

"You bet," Diane answered happily. She had been looking forward to this weekend at Clear Lake for weeks.

"Don't forget to pack your medicine," her mom reminded her. "I'm still not sure you're well enough to go."

"Mom, my cold is almost gone. I promise to stay warm."

Diane had worked hard to convince her parents that she

should be allowed to go on the trip. Mr. Carter, the science teacher, often took the Earth Science Club on field trips, but this would be the first time they were going to camp out. Besides, it was sort of a celebration, too. Until last year, Clear Lake had not deserved its name. It had been a dumping site for all sorts of trash, and who knows what else, from the nearby town. Diane's science club had been part of a special effort to stop the dumping and clean up the lake. Cold or no cold—this field trip was a must.

The trip up the mountain road took only a couple of hours. At the campsite, Mr. Carter and the eight kids quickly set up their tents. Since it was still early in the season, there were no other campers around, so the group had its choice of the best sites close to the lake.

"Who wants to go for a swim?" Paul Kelly called out, appearing at the opening to his tent wearing his swimsuit.

"That sounds like a great idea," Mr. Carter agreed. "But I have to gather some kindling and set up our fire pit first. I don't want anyone going into the water unless I'm with you."

Everyone groaned.

"I can find kindling," Diane chimed in. "I still have a cold, and can't go swimming."

"That's very nice of you, Diane," said Mr. Carter. "Okay, you're in charge of setting up the fire."

Within minutes, the rest of the group was splashing knee-deep in the cold water. Paul, Terry and Josh were the first to dive in. Each surfaced a few yards from shore, sputtering and shivering.

"It's not so cold out here," Terry lied. "C'mon!"

"Be careful," Mr. Carter warned. "The rocks on the

bottom are covered with algae and can be slippery."

"*Cool!*" Diane's best friend, Sara, said, slipping on her diving mask and snorkel. "I'll see what else is down there." She eased out a little deeper into the lake, studying the rocks beneath that were carpeted with delicate strands of algae. She dived down and picked up a long, flat rock to get a better look at it. Gripping it in one hand, she cringed when it started to wriggle. Then she felt a nip on her fingers, and the object squirmed out of her grasp. Sara's startled scream took the form of a stream of bubbles heading for the surface. She whirled in the water and followed the bubbles up. Then she swam for the shallows where Mr. Carter, Lisa and Bill were gathering water samples in jars.

"Mr. Carter!" Sara gasped, pushing her mask up to her forehead. "I picked up this rock and it was all slimy . . . it moved . . . it really did . . . and it bit me!" She held out her hand to show a tiny drop of blood at the tip of her finger.

"Calm down, Sara," the teacher said, soothingly. "The algae makes the rocks slippery. You probably just dropped it."

"No, sir." She shook her head. "It wiggled back and forth, trying to get away!"

Lisa looked up from filling a jar. "It was probably a fish—you know, one of those flatfish that live on the bottom. You just thought it was a rock."

"Flatfish don't usually bite," whined Sara. "And besides, it was covered all over with weird, stringy-looking algae."

"You mean like this?" Paul waded toward them. He was holding a handful of the slimy green stuff. Long strands of it dripped between his fingers. "What is it, Mr. Carter?"

The science teacher ripped off a bit of the weird plant

and looked at it very closely. "I'm not sure." He reached into his shoulder pack, took out a plastic box and put the small algae sample inside. "We'll take it back with us and try to find out what it is," he said, tucking the box into his pack.

"Look!" Sara pointed to where the bushes were growing right along the shoreline. "It's over there, too." Algae covered the lower branches of the bushes. Their leaves were furry with it, and strings of the emerald-colored slime clung to the branches that overhung the lake.

"That's strange," Lisa said. She stood up and sloshed toward the bushes. "It seems to be growing just as well *out* of the water as in it." As she stood examining the strands, something drifted out from under a branch and gently bumped her leg. "Gross!" she screamed and back-pedaled several steps. "Mr. Carter! Look at this!"

The body of a large dead duck was floating in the water. Most of its feathers were covered with a fine layer of algae. The longest strands hung from its open beak.

Bill whistled softly, "Wow, that stuff must grow fast. Do you think it's poison? Maybe the duck tried to eat it."

Mr. Carter shook his head, then looked at the lengthening shadows on the shore. "I don't know what to make of it. But I think it's best if we all get out of the water. We'll come back out in the morning." He rubbed his hands on his shorts. "And when we get back I'll warm up a tub of water. I want you all to wash your hands really well."

Paul nodded. "Yeah, this stuff is kind of sticky."

· · · · · · · · · ·

Excited from their adventure in the lake, the club members trooped into camp, laughing and chattering. Diane had gathered an impressive pile of kindling and had set up the fire pit. "How was the water?" she asked cheerily.

"Great," Josh answered. "Except for the attack of the mutant green slime." Everyone laughed.

Diane raised an eyebrow. "What do you mean?"

Josh grinned. "Nothing. There's just this strange stuff growing in the lake. After everything that was dumped in there over the years, it's no surprise."

"YUCK—and you were swimming in it!" Diane said, wrinkling up her nose. "Now I'm not sorry I didn't go. Anyway, the fire is ready to be lit."

"And you did a fine job," Mr. Carter added. "I don't know about all of you, but I'm hungry. Who wants to eat?"

The answer was a general cheer.

While the other kids changed into dry clothes, Diane scouted around the edge of the clearing for more wood. She noticed a small branch sticking out from under a clump of bushes. As she slid it out, a squirrel scurried out from under one of the bushes.

"Hi, little guy," she said. "I'm sorry if . . ."

Her words froze in her throat. The squirrel had turned and bared its long, chisel-like teeth at her. Then it made a strange hissing noise, as if it were trying to growl. Diane had never seen a squirrel behave like that. Even in the deepening shadows of twilight, she could see clearly enough to realize that she had never seen a squirrel that looked like this one, either. Its glistening fur was a patchwork of deep emerald green, and strands of slime hung loosely from its snout.

The small creature lunged. Diane jumped back and fell out of its way as it dashed back into the undergrowth.

"Wow," Diane whispered in awe. She stood up slowly, dusted herself off and decided not to mention the incident to the others. No one would believe that she had been attacked by a vicious green squirrel anyway.

· · · · · · · · · ·

By the time the full moon had risen, there was a blazing fire in the pit and everyone was roasting hot dogs. It was a clear,

crisp night, and Diane pushed any thoughts of the strange squirrel out of her mind—until Lisa mentioned the strange algae and the dead duck they had found floating in the lake.

"It wasn't like anything I've ever seen before," Lisa whispered. "The stuff seemed to be growing in patches. Yuck—I can't believe I touched it!" Absentmindedly, she reached down and scratched above her ankle, the spot where the duck had bumped into her. Something about Lisa's hand caught Diane's eye.

"What have you got under your fingernails?" she asked.

Lisa looked at her fingernails, then turned her leg toward the fire and slowly pulled up the pantleg of her jeans. Both girls gasped. A large patch of green fuzz covered the side of Lisa's calf and ankle. "Mr. Carter," Diane said, her voice quivering. "I think you should look at this."

The science teacher came over and knelt down to examine Lisa's leg. But just then, Paul jumped up and dropped his hot dog into the fire. "Look!" The palms of both his hands were covered with fine green strands, and there were green stains between his fingers. Even as they all watched, the stains became slightly fuzzy. Paul grabbed a handful of dirt and rubbed his hands together frantically. "What is it, Mr. Carter? It hurts!" he wailed.

Lisa rubbed at her leg. Sara started to cry when she, too, found large greenish stains forming on her hands.

"Don't panic!" Mr. Carter tried to calm them. "It must be some kind of allergic reaction. I have some medication that should help." He grabbed his shoulder pack and flipped open the top. Inside, the plastic sample box had come open, and everything was covered with slimy green algae. "What the . . . ?" Mr. Carter dropped the bag and began to rub at his own hands. Dark stains were spreading up his arms. "I don't know what's going on here, but we need help. Everybody get into the van. We've got to get into town. The keys . . ." He felt in his pockets.

Diane could tell from his voice that something was terribly wrong with him. He was losing control.

"Where are the keys?" he screamed. "They must be in here!" He picked up the shoulder pack, turned it over and dumped the contents on the ground. Like everything else, the keys to the van were coated with slime. Mr. Carter dropped to his knees and grabbed for them in the dirt, but before he could reach them, Sara kicked the keys into the fire.

"Mr. Carter!" Diane screamed, pointing at Sara. "What's happening to her?"

Sara stood grinning beside the fire. Long strands of green slime hung from her lips. When she opened her mouth to speak, she sputtered and drooled. The slime was obviously growing inside of her mouth, too.

"*Nothing* is happening to me," Sara said, turning to face Diane. "Or at least nothing that concerns you . . . yet. But I can fix that!" She reached out her ooze-covered hand.

Diane squirmed away while the other kids gathered behind Sara. Diane looked from one to the other. Every one of them was spotted with large patches of the grotesque green stuff. The rancid odor stung Diane's nostrils. Tears filled her eyes. "Sara, you're my best friend. What are you doing?"

"I just want to hold hands, *friend.*"

Diane moaned, "What is wrong with you? With *all* of you?"

"Stop whining, you little brat!" Mr. Carter stood up and shuffled toward her. In the firelight she could see that he was baring his teeth, now sharp and pointed like the squirrel's had been.

"This slime, whatever it is, it's changing you," Diane sobbed. "I'll get help." She scrambled to her feet and backed away toward the forest. "I can make it to town. It's not so far," she continued to babble, as they all moved closer and closer to her. "I'll get you help."

Suddenly, a form grabbed at her from the shadows. "Who says we *want* help?" A slime-covered being snarled with what sounded like Josh's voice.

47

Diane twisted away from its grasp. Stumbling and crying she raced into the forest. Twigs and branches seemed to reach out for her. They scraped at her face and hands as she lurched forward. She could hear the others following close behind. Which way was the main road?

In the pale moonlight, she saw a clearing ahead and changed course toward it. She ran out into the open space and stood gasping for air. Suddenly, there was a screech from above, and a creature dived at her from the sky. The horrible slime dripped from its widespread wings and sharp talons, which Diane barely managed to dodge. Only the creature's glowing eyes were free of the stuff. From its piercing cry, she could tell the thing had once been an owl. It turned to attack again, and Diane ducked back into the trees.

She waited until the screeches finally died away. The silence settled in like a fog, and the entire forest seemed to press close around her. "Where are they?" she whispered. Then she caught a scent on the air. It was a dank, musty smell, and it was growing stronger. Then she saw something glinting through the leaves just a few yards away. It was the remains of their campfire. "I've doubled back to the lake," she moaned.

Diane edged around the dense vegetation and neared the rocky shore. Now she could hear the low growls of the monsters that had once been her friends. They were coming closer.

Frantically, she looked from side to side. There was nowhere to run. She glanced fearfully at the calm water. They had said the slime was in the water, but that was further down the shore. Maybe the lake was all right here.

Step by step, she carefully worked her way over the rocks and eased into the icy lake up to her knees. The water glittered in the moonlight. It didn't *feel* slippery.

The sound of something heavy lumbering over the rocks forced her to make a decision. She silently slipped under the overhanging branches and hid among the shadows. The water, now up to her neck, was so cold that it was painful, but she bit her lip and didn't make a sound.

Snuffling and grunting, several of the horrid creatures limped along the shore. They seemed to be communicating with one another, but no human sound emerged. Diane shrank back into the darkness. Her heart was pounding so hard that she was afraid they might hear it. One of the creatures stepped close enough that she could have reached out and touched its slime-slick leg. Diane held her breath and squeezed her eyes shut. She was barely aware of the low-growing leaves and twigs that scratched her face as she withdrew further among the branches.

Finally, the hideous beasts hobbled away over the rocks. Diane waited until everything was silent, then she groped her way out of the water. Her feet were almost numb with the cold, but she ran. Within moments she stumbled out onto the narrow dirt road that the group had traveled to reach the campsite. She raced downhill and finally reached the main highway. Every breath was agony as she continued to flee down the center of the pavement, afraid to wander too near to the dense forest on either side. She knew only too well what terrible secrets the trees were hiding.

All at once she realized that there was something behind her, something drawing near. She whirled around and stared into what looked like two huge, gleaming eyes.

"Miss . . . wait. Don't be afraid. What are you doing out here alone?" The owner of the voice stepped closer. Diane was able to make out a tall woman in a uniform. The gleaming eyes were the headlights of a car. She felt faint, and sensed the ground under her feet starting to spin. A moment later someone was wrapping a jacket around her and helping her into a car. As her head cleared she realized that it was a highway patrol car. The officer who was driving was speaking into the mouthpiece of his police radio.

"I don't know," he was saying. "Her clothes are all damp. I imagine she's been in the lake. We'll bring her in first, then head on back to check whether anyone else is around." He finished his call and looked into his rearview mirror at Diane. "Well, young lady, are you feeling okay? Can you tell us what happened to you?"

Diane opened her mouth, but she couldn't seem to make a sound. "Don't worry, honey," the female officer said kindly. "Whatever happened, you're safe now." The woman reached under her seat, pulled out a small bag and fished out a compact and some tissues. "Here you go. Dry your eyes, and try to rub some of that dirt from your face. It will make you feel better. We'll be in town in a few minutes."

Diane took the tissues and dabbed at her eyes. Opening the lighted compact, she began to clear the dirt from her face. Then she felt a low scream rising in her throat. She rubbed harder and harder at the dark, greenish stain on her cheek, but it wouldn't go away. It only got bigger and bigger.

The Storm

lay Davis opened the map. "I think we missed the turnoff, Dad." He looked up at a sign as they zipped past it. "I think we should have gotten off about a mile back."

Clay's mother turned from the front passenger seat and pointed to the map. "May I see that, please?"

Clay refolded the map and handed it to her. She studied the map for a moment in the failing afternoon light.

"He's right," she said finally.

"Oh, great!" Jessica, Clay's older sister, groaned. She looked out at the gray, leaden sky as raindrops began to splat against the windshield. "Now we're never going to get

51

there," she whined. "Who picked this old inn in the middle of the boondocks, anyway?"

"You did!" everyone chimed in.

"Oh . . . right." Jessica grinned sheepishly. "I thought it would be romantic. It's almost a century old."

"Yeah," Clay said, "and if we don't get there soon, *we'll* be a century old!"

"Don't worry," their dad said as he maneuvered the van into the right lane. "We'll take the next exit and double back."

• • • • • • • • • •

More than an hour later, after several wrong turns and some rough roads, Mr. Davis guided the family van over a rickety bridge across a rain-swollen stream. Through the trees, a small village came into view. In the drizzling rain and gathering darkness, the scene looked eerie and uninviting.

The stores lining the main street were all closed. The village appeared forsaken. Jessica was the first to say what everyone else was thinking. "Maybe this wasn't such a good idea. That Traveler's Rest Motel back by the expressway didn't look so bad. Maybe we should stay there."

"I'm afraid we don't have a choice." Mr. Davis looked down at the glow of the gauges on the dash. "We don't have much gas left and it looks as though that closed gas station over there is the only one in town. Besides, I don't think it would be smart to drive around anymore on these back roads in the rain. Let's just try to find the inn and stay for tonight. If we don't like it, we can leave in the morning."

The rain pelted the windshield. No one spoke as Mr. Davis inched the van down the empty, dismal main street.

Clay had the strange feeling that the village wasn't deserted at all. He squinted out into the gloom of nightfall, certain that someone out there was watching them pass. A cold chill made him shiver.

"You know what it means when you shiver?" Jessica said. "It means that someone in the future has just walked across your grave."

Clay elbowed her playfully. "No, it doesn't. It means . . ."

"Look! There's a light," Mrs. Davis interrupted. "That must be it." Through the heavy rain they could see a dim glow a few hundred yards up on a hillside. Mr. Davis turned at the next corner and headed up the slick hill, then parked. A sudden flash of lightning crackled across the sky, and for a moment the landscape was bathed in a ghostly light. An old Victorian building was hunched against the forested hillside. Dense clumps of trees and bushes seemed to be pressing in around the inn, as if they were trying to push it from its unsteady perch.

Mrs. Davis took a deep breath. "Well, there's no sense sitting out here in the rain. Let's make a run for it."

Clay slipped his arms through the straps of his backpack. "Last one in is a drowned rat!" he yelled, slamming the door behind him and running through the pelting rain toward the lighted porch. Laughing, he clambered up the wooden steps and under the shelter of the overhang. When he turned to watch the rest of the family struggle across the muddy path, something at the corner of the building caught his eye. A figure (a girl?) slipped from the edge of the porch into the darkness. But that was impossible. Who, or what, would go out into such a storm? Still, something about what he had seen seemed oddly familiar to Clay. Suddenly, he became aware of his dad behind him, holding open the door to the inn.

"C'mon, son. This is no time to daydream."

Clay moved toward the door, taking one last look over his shoulder. Shrugging, he stepped inside and was a little startled by the light. The entry hall was warm and cheerful—not what he had expected. A pleasant, gray-haired woman in a crisp flowered dress greeted them.

"Oh, good heavens," she declared. "This is not any sort of night for anyone to be traveling. Come in, come in. There's a warm fire in the parlor. I'm Mrs. Reese . . . Ellen. Welcome to Dark Acres Inn. I'm afraid we didn't think you were going to make it tonight, so I don't have dinner prepared, but I can put together a warm snack in no time."

"A snack sounds great," said Mrs. Davis. "But could we go to our rooms first and change out of these damp clothes?"

"Oh, gracious, yes. I did prepare rooms just in case. Three, right? My husband will get you settled. Albert!" she called. "Our guests have arrived."

Albert, a tall, kind-faced man with a head of thick, white hair, sauntered in and helped the Davises with their bags.

"Do you have a granddaughter?" Clay asked.

The man tilted his head. "No. What makes you ask?"

Clay motioned toward the door. "When I was outside, I thought I saw someone step off the porch. I thought maybe it was your granddaughter or something."

The two older people glanced at each other quickly. Clay

noticed Mrs. Reese nervously fingering the lacy collar of her dress. "Sometimes the lightning can play tricks . . . it can make you think you see things that aren't there."

Mr. Reese picked up some luggage. "Now, it wouldn't be hospitable for us to let you catch cold. Just follow me, and we'll get you all set." He guided them along the hallway and opened the doors to three rooms. "If you don't like these, you can take your pick of the rest," he said pleasantly. "There's no one else here."

"These rooms will be fine," said Mr. Davis. "We'll join you and your wife in the parlor shortly."

Once Clay was alone, he dropped his backpack onto a chair and unzipped it. He pulled out a dry sweatshirt, jeans, sneakers and socks, but he didn't change right away. Instead, he clicked off the light and stood at the window, staring out into the night. Outside, tree branches tossed violently in the rising wind. Lightning flashed. "No one could be out there on a night like this," he whispered to himself, then switched the light back on and quickly changed clothes.

But when he looked into the mirror to comb his damp hair, he froze. In the reflection, he could see the window behind him. The sad eyes of a pale young girl gazed steadily in at him from outside. Slowly she raised her tiny, clenched hand and began to knock on the glass.

Clay dropped the comb and whirled around to face the window, but now there was nothing but a wind-whipped branch beating against the glass. Another flash of lightning lit up the empty scene, and Clay bolted out of the room and headed down to the parlor. As he reached the entryway, he slowed down. How would he explain what he had seen? He

didn't want everyone to think he was just a scared kid. Maybe it was just a trick of the light.

By the time he joined his family and the Reeses, Clay had almost convinced himself that nothing had happened . . . until he saw Jessica's face. She kept glancing at the French doors, which appeared to lead to an outside terrace.

Clay's dad smiled at him. "What took you so long? Mr. Reese was just telling us a little about the area. There's a dam up at the top of this valley with a lake behind it. If it stops raining tomorrow, maybe we can go up and have a picnic."

"Sounds great, Dad," Clay answered, but like Jessica, he couldn't stop looking at the French doors. They seemed so fragile. If there really were something outside, those doors didn't seem strong enough to keep it out.

Clay accepted a sandwich and a steaming cup of hot soup from Mrs. Reese, then sat by the fire near his sister. As the adults continued their conversation, he whispered to her, "Did you see anything strange tonight?"

Wide-eyed, she looked at him. "No. Well . . . not exactly. That is, it wasn't that I *saw* anything, but when I was in my room I had this spooky feeling that I was being watched. I don't like this place. Did *you* see anything?"

Clay decided not to make his sister any more frightened than she was. "No," he lied. "It's just weird here."

Jessica's hand shook as she reached for her cup. "This place is so old. Do you think it could be haunted?" Her gaze flickered toward the French doors. "I feel like we're not as alone here as we think."

• • • • • • • • •

After they had eaten, the family retired to their rooms. Despite the strange happenings, Clay soon fell sound asleep. But whatever was haunting his waking thoughts seemed to have found its way into his dreams as well.

At first, his dream was pleasant. He was in a field near the inn on a warm summer day. He could feel the sun on his face and hear the laughter of a young girl. She began to sing a familiar song, but after a moment or two the song turned to a kind of moan, almost like the sound of the wind. The moan rose to a cry . . . a cry for help. He tried to reach the girl, but the ground turned to thick mud. He was sinking deeper and deeper, until finally he couldn't breathe. All the while he could hear cries and sobbing, but they were the cries of many people . . . people in terror.

Clay sat up, fully awake, and gaped out the window directly into a pair of mournful eyes. Once again, he saw the ashen face of the girl he'd seen earlier. She opened her mouth as if to speak, but Clay heard only the crash of thunder. The girl curled her fingers at the base of the window, trying to open it, and then her eyes met Clay's again.

As if still in a dream, Clay felt the need to do what the strange girl wanted. He kicked away the blankets, rose slowly, and moved toward the window. The girl's eyes glittered as Clay touched the metal latch. Suddenly, a bolt of lightning lit up the sky, and Clay saw that there were dozens of "people" outside in the storm. They were all dressed in turn-of-the-century clothes, and they were moving toward the inn as if their feet weren't quite touching the ground. A tremendous crack of thunder drowned out Clay's scream as he backed away, turned and raced into the hall. He screamed again as he crashed into his sister. She was shaking violently.

"There's something out there, Clay!"

"I saw them, too! We've got to get Mom and Dad!" He flung open the door to his parents' room but it was empty.

Clay and Jessica ran down the hall. Relief washed over them when they saw their parents sitting in the parlor, but their relief lasted for only a moment. When Mr. Davis looked up, his face was strained. Mr. Reese was twisting the dials on a radio, but all it was receiving was static.

"Come on in, kids." Mr. Davis motioned to them. "You might as well know what's going on. It seems that all this rain has weakened the dam. There have been reports on the radio that everyone down below has been evacuated, but the stream has flooded out the road. There's no way we can get out." He smiled to reassure them. "But Mr. Reese says we're on high ground and we shouldn't be in danger."

Mrs. Davis studied Clay's face, then Jessica's. "There's something else wrong. What's the matter?"

Clay glanced at his sister. "We saw something . . . people . . . outside. They were dressed weird. Like out of the history books. They were all around the inn."

Mr. Reese shut the radio off. Mrs. Reese finally broke the silence. "It's them, Albert. They're here for us."

"What is she talking about?" Mrs. Davis demanded.

Albert Reese rubbed his eyes and smoothed back his hair with both hands. "Nothing. It's just an old story."

"Tell them, Albert, or I will," the old woman said.

Mr. Reese began speaking slowly. "This isn't the first inn to stand on this site. There was another one before the flood of 1885. A fine man and his wife ran it. They had a little girl

59

and boy. Those kids were never apart. Then came the storm. It was as bad as this one, or worse. The townsfolk down below were worried about the dam. Word is, they took shelter up here, but it didn't do them any good."

Mrs. Reese walked to the fireplace. She took down a photograph from among the many on the mantelpiece.

Mr. Reese continued the story. "Seems the dam did break, and it was worse than anybody thought it would be. The water raged down this valley with a vengeance. It washed away the inn. Nobody survived."

He sighed heavily. "Some folks think that when people die violently like that, they don't rest. Some folks here in the valley say that when it rains they can hear the moans of the dead on the wind. But those were good, hardworking people. I don't see why they would want to harm anyone."

"You're not telling me you believe in ghosts?!" Mr. Davis asked with surprise.

"I grew up around here," the old man answered. "There have been times when the rain was real bad and the wind howled through the trees like . . . well, I'm not one to scoff."

"This is the family that owned the inn." Mrs. Reese turned the photograph so the others could see it. It was of a man and woman in turn-of-the-century clothes. Seated in front of them were a boy and girl holding hands.

"Oh, my goodness!" Jessica gasped. "Clay, the boy looks just like you!"

Clay said nothing. He stared at the face of the girl. It was the same face that had gazed in the window at him.

A bolt of lightning crackled. Seconds later, thunder shook the inn as if it were trying to pound it to the ground.

The lights went dead, leaving the parlor lit only by the flickering fire. A tremendous gust of wind crashed open the French doors and rain poured in, but no one moved to close them: standing just beyond the entrance was something that had once been a little girl. Her dull blond curls hung limply around her pale face, and her sodden dress was streaked with mud. A few yards away, on either side of her, were others who appeared to have shared her fate.

The girl's eyes were locked onto Clay's as she raised her small hand and motioned for him to follow her. Without thinking, he began to walk toward the doorway.

"Clay! No!" His mother grabbed at him, but he quickly slipped into the downpour. The wind ripped at his clothes and the rain drenched him, but he was no longer in control. He *had* to go with her. Slipping and sliding in the mud, he struggled up the hillside after the phantom girl.

"We've got to stop him! Clay!" His mother screamed.

"Come on," Mr. Reese said to Mr. Davis. "We'll stop him." The two men ran out into the downpour. At that moment the front door to the inn slammed open. Seeming to float just above the ground, several figures entered and drifted toward the parlor.

Jessica shrieked. "Mom, what are they? What do they want?" In terror she clutched at her mother. Mrs. Davis picked up a lamp from the table and threw it at the specters, but they kept advancing. The air became thick with the smell of damp earth and mildew.

"We've got to get out," said Mrs. Reese, shaking with fear. She snatched a blanket from the arm of the couch and threw it around Jessica's shoulders. The two women and

Jessica ran into the storm after the others. Driven by fear, they climbed higher up the slick hillside.

Far above, Clay stumbled to his knees. He tried to get up again but realized that something had him by the ankle. The rain had eased and the sky had begun to lighten with the approaching dawn. Clay looked down and saw that it was his father who was gripping him tightly. "No, Dad!" he squirmed. "Let me go. I've got to go to her."

Suddenly, Clay heard distant thunder, and at the same time he realized that the ground was shaking. The roaring grew louder as Mrs. Reese, Mrs. Davis and Jessica scrambled up the hill. Seconds later, a raging wall of water tore through the valley below. It ripped up trees and sent boulders flying. The mud-choked waters fell upon the inn like a savage beast and ripped it to pieces, carrying away what was left.

The six people huddled against the hillside, safe from the deluge. The phantoms stood below at the edge of the water, and as the day grew brighter, they faded into the flood, one by one.

"Saints preserve us," Mrs. Reese said, holding on to her husband. "If it hadn't been for them, we would have been in that building." Clay looked up at the fading form of the girl above him. She held out her hand and smiled. He reached out and brushed her fingertips just before she vanished.

"Thank you," he whispered, hoping that she could hear him.

Homecoming

he call of an owl woke Timothy. It took a long time for him to draw himself from sleep. When he did, he was groggy and confused. He licked his lips. They were dry, and his tongue felt thick and clumsy. He blinked at the darkness around him. *Why was it so cold?* He reached for the blankets to pull them around his shoulders, but all he managed to grasp was a handful of dry, crackling leaves. With great effort, he sat up and looked around.

It was easy to see that he wasn't home in bed. He had been lying on the cold, hard ground. Windblown leaves were scattered across his bare legs and feet, and a few had lodged themselves in the tatters of his clothes and the tangles of his uncombed hair. His hair—why was it so long? And why was it so cold for a summer night?

"Where am I?" he said aloud. The sound of his own voice startled him and he felt the first pangs of fear crawl up his spine.

WHOOOOO! WHOOOOO! The hoot of the owl that had awakened him made him jump and he twisted around to find where it was coming from. Low in the branches of a nearby tree, a pair of round eyes glowed in the moonlight.

WHOOOOO! WHOOOOO! It called again. Then another glint of light caught Timothy's attention. Painfully, he stood and shuffled toward it. His legs were stiff, and he felt the cold down to his bones. He tried to move quietly, afraid of what might be waiting on the other side of the branches. Finally, he pushed aside a scraggly twig and stepped into the open.

Stretched in front of him were the dark waters of a lake. A wide, rippling ribbon of moonlight cut across the center of it. Timothy could hear the water lapping gently on the shore and a light, chilly breeze stirred the leaves on the ground around him. It also stirred a memory.

"The lake," he said to himself. "We were playing . . . Sandy? Where are you?" he called. She was his cousin and they had been playing near the water. His mom had asked them to be home before dark . . . HOME!

A sharp pang shot through Timothy's heart as he thought of his home and of his room, with all the posters of sailboats. That was why he was here! He and Sandy had come to the lake to test out a new model boat they had built. The boat had drifted off, and they had followed it along the shoreline, trying to catch up to it. By the time they had found it, trapped in a tangle of bushes overhanging the water, the setting sun was turning the sky a deep, dark red.

Timothy could still hear the sound of his mother's voice warning them, "Now don't stay out too late," she had said. "I don't want you walking home in the dark."

"Aw, come on, Mom," he had grumbled. "What are you worried about? I'd know my way through the woods even if it was pitch-black."

"What did I just say, Timothy?" she had said sternly.

"Be home before dark. Oh, okay," he'd agreed reluctantly as he ran outside to meet Sandy.

"Take an apple with you." He remembered his mom calling after him. "You'll get hungry out there."

• • • • • • • • •

And his mother was right. He was hungry . . . *very* hungry . . . but it wasn't an apple that he wanted. It was something else, something he couldn't quite think of. His mother had also been right about how dangerous it was to stay out after dark. Somehow Timothy had gotten lost. And Sandy— where was she? Timothy recalled standing on the lakeshore with her as the sun sank below the horizon.

"It's getting dark fast," he had said. "We'll get home faster if we cut through the woods."

Sandy had shaken her head. "No, Timmy. I really don't want to. It's too creepy."

"You're such a scaredy-cat!" He had made fun of her.

They had been close for as long as he could remember. When Sandy's parents were killed in a car accident, she had come to live with Timothy and his parents. They were a lot alike, except for one thing. He didn't really mind the dark, and Sandy was afraid of it—*really* afraid. She was certain that ghosts, werewolves and vampires actually existed. Timothy thought of how frightened she had been when they had first headed into the trees. Now he was sorry he had made fun of her, especially since he didn't know where she was.

"Somebody must be looking for us," he whispered to no one. He looked up and down the moonlit shoreline. "They're probably looking in the woods. I'll just cut through and head home. They've probably found Sandy; now they'll find me." He babbled on and on to himself as he rambled toward the trees, their leafless branches forming a dark tangle of shadows.

He walked into the dense forest. The echo of his footsteps made it sound as though there were *things* slinking through the woods. The wind softly rocked the bare branches above and seemed to whisper a warning: *Go back! Go back!* But Timothy forced himself on. Some buried thought kept nagging at him . . . but all he could think about was how cold he was, and how very, very hungry.

Maybe Sandy was nearby, all alone and frightened. He stopped and called her name. A rustling noise came from somewhere in the dark behind him. Was it her? He strained to hear, but again there was only silence.

Then out of the corner of his eye, Timothy caught a glimpse of a pale glimmer. He snapped his gaze to a clump of trees just ahead. A memory stirred. That was where they had first seen the woman! Timothy felt his insides twist in fear as he thought of her. She had been standing in a shadow, staring at them. Sandy had noticed her first.

"Timmy!" she had cried out. "Look! Someone's there!"

Timothy had tried to put on a brave act. "Maybe you were right," he had said to Sandy. "Maybe we should go back and walk home along the shore."

The woman had moved toward them. As she'd stepped from the shadows, Timothy had seen her face and gasped in horror. She was as pale as chalk, but her eyes were gleaming like bloodred coals. Her lips were curled back in a hideous grin. Timothy would never forget the sight of the gleaming fangs that protruded from her mouth.

"Run! Run for the lake!" he screamed at Sandy, pushing her ahead of him.

· · · · · · · · · ·

Timothy remembered racing through the woods in terror. He could still feel his heart pumping, the bushes scratching at his legs. He could still feel himself tumbling as his foot caught on a fallen branch. He had landed hard and had the wind knocked out of him. The last thing he remembered was watching Sandy running away, and for a moment he was angry at her for leaving him. For just a split second, Timothy felt that he wanted to pay her back for leaving him alone in this horrible forest of tall, scary trees.

"The trees!" Timothy gasped. He looked up in realization. The summer leaves were gone. Why hadn't he noticed that before? How long had he been out here? He

began to run. Was that horrible woman still out here? He had to get home. He was so cold, and terribly hungry. And the shadows—they crouched on every side as though they cloaked some secret horror! Timothy forced his feet to move. From all directions he could hear the rustling of dry leaves stirred by the cold wind. He imagined bloodred eyes watching his every step. He was not alone. He could sense it.

Suddenly, he burst from the forest into a clearing. Down the hill and to his right he could see the lake again. It was a dark tongue of water with lights glittering at its tip—the lights of town . . . and home.

Timothy stumbled down the slope, but as he neared the familiar place he felt a growing sense of dread. Without knowing why, he stayed in the shadows. He was becoming more at ease in the dark, and the cold no longer bothered him. When he turned onto his own street he noticed that the houses were strung with colored lights. It was a holiday of some sort, but that didn't seem important. All that was important was the gnawing hunger that was growing in him with each passing moment. There were no colored lights on his own house, but there was a warm glow coming from the front window. Someone was home.

Timothy no longer felt any fear. He moved quietly toward the window and peered in. The light hurt his eyes.

Sandy was at the edge of the couch near the fireplace, her head resting on a pillow. Her eyes were closed and a book lay across her lap. For a moment, as Timothy stared in at her, he again felt a moment of anger . . . but the feeling was soon replaced by hunger. He had to eat . . . soon. He slipped his thin, pale fingers under the window and pushed, and it slid up easily. Then, soundlessly, he pulled himself up to the ledge and eased over the windowsill.

The room felt hot and stuffy. He wanted to escape into the safety of the cool night. That horrible gnawing in his stomach was relentless. He *needed* something to eat. Leaving a trail of dried dirt and leaves, he scraped across the floor to stand behind his cousin. A lock of her hair was draped across her neck, and he gently pushed it away. Her eyes fluttered open.

"Sandy," he moaned hoarsely. "I'm home."

Sandy's eyes widened in terror. "No—OH, NO!" she screamed. "It can't be! You're . . . !" Her eyes rolled up and she became limp.

Timothy gripped her neck in his chalk-white fingers. It was so warm, and he was so hungry. He drew back his lips and ran his tongue over his sharp teeth.

"It's good to be back, cousin," he snarled. Then, scanning the room, Timothy noticed a photograph of himself. The frame was draped in black, with an inscription that read "In loving memory." He smiled slightly, touched by the sentiment.

"You'll have to forgive me if I eat and run," he said, baring his fangs and sinking them into his cousin's neck.

Outside the window a woman with bloodred eyes watched. "Very good, my new little friend," she whispered. "Very good."

Portrait of Evil

ndrea had always dreamed of having her own horse. Now her dream was almost coming true. She wasn't going to own a horse, but at least she was going to spend a whole summer at a ranch.

Her Aunt Joanne and Uncle Charles had agreed that she could stay with them while her parents were in Europe. Andrea loved staying with her aunt and uncle. There was always something fun to do at the Red Mesa Ranch, named for the tall, flat-topped cliffs that rose along the east edge of the ranch. Uncle Charles raised horses, and her Aunt Joanne was an art collector and an artist.

Now looking down from the window of the plane as the

late afternoon shadows deepened across the mountains and desert below, Andrea was filled with excitement.

Once in the terminal she found her aunt and uncle waiting at the gate. Aunt Joanne was all smiles. "We are so glad you're finally here!" she exclaimed.

"Me, too." Andrea grinned widely as she gave her aunt and uncle a hug.

A half hour later, Uncle Charles pulled the van onto a wide dirt road that led to the ranch. Instead of going straight to the house, though, he headed toward the corral.

"I have something I want to show you," he said to Andrea. As he stopped the van next to the fence, a young boy led a beautiful bay mare into the corral.

"Is she for me?" Andrea said in a tiny voice.

"She sure is," Uncle Charles laughed. "Her name is Monterey. Why don't you go over and let Jesse introduce you?" he said, gesturing to a tall, thin boy holding the reins. "We'll take your bags into the house."

Andrea gave her aunt and uncle huge hugs, then raced into the corral. "Hi," she said grinning at Jesse. He appeared to be only a little older than she was. "I guess you're Jesse. I'm Andrea. Do you take care of the horses?"

He smiled back at her. "Sort of. My dad is the foreman here. I help out when I don't have school."

"You're so lucky. I just love horses." She gently petted the mare's neck. "This is going to be the best summer. Maybe I'll even take my first ride after dinner tonight."

Andrea noticed Jesse's smile falter. "You'd best wait until the morning. It isn't safe."

"What do you mean?" she asked. "Why isn't it safe?"

He looked out toward the desert, engulfed in shadow. In the distance the first lights were winking on in town. "The desert may look empty, but it isn't. There are things out there that are better left alone. I'll put Monterey in the barn. Then I'll walk you to the main house."

At dinner that night Andrea asked Aunt Joanne about the strange thing that Jesse had said.

"He seemed nervous. Is something wrong?" she asked.

Aunt Joanne ran her finger slowly over a pattern in the tablecloth as if she were thinking about something, then she finally spoke. "About two hundred years ago this valley was part of a Spanish land grant to a man named Don Ramon Hidalgo. Apparently he wasn't a very nice person."

Uncle Charles broke in. "That's putting it mildly. It seems he brutally ended the lives of a number of people, including his own sister. He also reportedly dabbled in sorcery. Anyway, he was finally hanged, but the people around here are a superstitious lot. They blame anything bad that happens on Don Hidalgo. Of course it's nonsense. Jesse is just being foolish."

"Charles," Aunt Joanne said sternly. "Jesse has lived here all of his life. These legends are a part of the land, and you must admit that lately there have been some . . . accidents. I think we should take his concerns seriously."

"Oh, really?" The corner of Uncle Charles's mouth turned up in a half smile. "If you think that we have anything to worry about from old Don Hidalgo, then why do you have him hanging in your studio?"

"WHAT!" Andrea exclaimed.

"No, no, dear," Aunt Joanne laughed. "*He* isn't hanging.

It's just a portrait of him." She lifted one eyebrow and looked at her husband. "It is from the original Hidalgo collection. I found it in a gallery in Albuquerque just three months ago. I also found some old books that belonged to the infamous Don Hidalgo himself. They're in the library. I'll show them to you sometime if you like. But enough about this. I made a special dessert and it's time to serve it."

After dinner Andrea helped to clear the table, then asked to be excused. She wanted to take a look at the portrait of Don Hidalgo in her aunt's art studio. She had expected a somber picture of a man standing alone. But the portrait was very large, and there were at least a dozen people and several horses in the painting, too. She studied the scene carefully. Her eye was drawn to the man at the center of the group. Looking at him made her shiver. There were deep lines around the mouth that gave it a hard, cruel look. The cold, dark eyes lacked any trace of humanity.

The next morning Andrea was at the corral before breakfast. Jesse helped her saddle Monterey, and then he saddled his own horse, Thunder, and guided Andrea on a riding tour of the foothills. Finally, when they were riding toward home, Andrea asked Jesse about the legend.

"My aunt told me the story," she said. "It sounds weird. Why are people still frightened of a dead man?"

Jesse sighed. "For two hundred years this valley has suffered. People have died in strange accidents, or have simply disappeared. All the while, strange sounds and lights have come from the Hidalgo mansion, even though it was supposed to be deserted. Finally, the house was torn down and the things in it were sold.

"For a time it seemed that the curse had ended. Then, about three months ago, a little girl disappeared from a local campsite. A month later another child vanished. They haven't been found. And, last month, the Peterson home burst into flames in the middle of the night. No one got out."

Andrea's thoughts were racing. "Did you say the first little girl disappeared three months ago?" she asked.

Jesse nodded. "Yeah, why?"

"The painting," she murmured. "That's when Aunt Joanne brought home the painting."

As soon as she got back to the ranch, Andrea went straight to her aunt's studio. In the morning light the face of Don Hidalgo looked even more grim. She studied the other figures. There were several children. One of the women was holding a little girl with curly, blonde hair who looked very out of place. There was something about the little girl's clothes that bothered her. For a moment Andrea thought of telling her fears to Uncle Charles, but that seemed silly. It was just a painting. It couldn't have any effect on the real world.

• • • • • • • • • •

Andrea had planned to ride again in the afternoon. Jesse was in town with his dad, but she felt comfortable with Monterey and so she set out on her own. She was an excellent rider and guided Monterey easily to a rise overlooking the valley. The view was beautiful. She rode for several miles, then decided to head back while it was still light.

Gently tugging on the reins, Andrea coaxed Monterey into a wide turn. That was when she noticed the other horse. It was standing alone near the edge of the cliff, a beautiful silhouette against the afternoon sky. Strangely, though, it seemed to be staring right at her. Then it started to move toward her. Andrea made a clicking noise and urged Monterey to a trot. The black horse increased its speed and began to close the distance between them. In alarm, Andrea loosened her grip on the reins. Monterey sensed her command and leaped forward in a full gallop. Desert sand flew up in huge chunks as Andrea's horse seemed to fly across the ground, trying to outdistance the pursuing stranger.

The black horse was cutting across at an angle toward them, forcing them to ride along the cliff. Eyes wide with fear, Monterey galloped closer and closer to the edge. Andrea leaned into her horse's body and tried to match her movement. Still, the black horse was closing the gap. Monterey's hooves dislodged rocks. Avalanches of sand and pebbles careened down the steep sides of the ledge. The black horse was almost on them! Andrea could hear its deep, heaving breaths. She could see its flaring nostrils and the splash of white on its forehead.

With a final effort, Monterey twisted away from the cliff to safer ground. Andrea suddenly became aware that they were no longer being followed. She pulled up on the reins. Tossing her head, Monterey slowed and stopped. They were alone. Andrea could see for miles around, but the black horse had disappeared.

Jesse met Andrea as she rode into the corral. "What have you been doing? This horse is exhausted," he said angrily.

"I know," Andrea gasped. "We were chased by a strange horse up near the rise. It tried to force us over the cliff!"

"A strange horse?" Jesse asked. "Why would a horse chase you?"

Andrea shook her head. "I'm not sure, but I think I've seen it somewhere before. It had a white blaze on its forehead."

"Look," Jesse said, holding the reins as Andrea slipped from the saddle. "You shouldn't go off riding on your own. Your aunt and uncle would be very upset."

Andrea set her mouth in a firm line. "I have to check something. Will you take care of Monterey for me?"

Moments later, she stood before the painting in her aunt's studio. It was just as she had remembered: the black horse with the white blaze was standing in the background. There was only one difference. Now, as nightfall came upon the ranch, the horse's coat appeared to be glistening with sweat.

Uncle Charles was in the library reading the afternoon paper. He looked up when Andrea knocked at the open door.

"I know you won't believe this," she began slowly. "But please listen. I think that the accidents that have been happening . . . the disappearances . . . I think they all have something to do with Don Hidalgo."

"Now, Andy," her uncle frowned. "There is certainly something serious going on here and everyone is worried, but it is a job for the police. It doesn't do any good to start blaming someone who died almost two centuries ago."

Andrea's gaze fell on the paper in Uncle Charles's hand. At the top of the page were pictures of the two missing children. "He may be dead, Uncle Charles," Andrea said earnestly, "but Don Hidalgo isn't gone. Please, come with me and bring the newspaper. I want to show you something."

Reluctantly, Uncle Charles followed Andrea into Aunt Joanne's studio. To his amazement, he, too, saw that the little blonde girl in the painting resembled one of the pictures in the paper. The painted face of another child seemed to look vaguely like the second missing youngster.

"I don't know what's going on here," Uncle Charles said worriedly, "but I think the sheriff should take a look at this." He picked up the phone and punched in a number. Andrea listened as he asked for the sheriff, then left a message. He slowly hung up the phone and turned to Andrea. "There's some trouble over at the Mendez place. The sheriff may not be back for a while. We'll have to wait. If he doesn't get back to us tonight, I'll reach him first thing in the morning."

• • • • • • • • • •

Andrea awoke to a frantic knock on her door. It was Aunt Joanne. She was trying to control tears and the shaking in her voice. "Andy, honey. There's been an accident."

Andrea knew immediately. "It's Uncles Charles, isn't it? What's happened?"

"I don't really know. It's so crazy. He wasn't around

when I got up this morning. At first I didn't think . . ." She began to sob. "If only I'd looked for him sooner. He must have been out there half the night."

"Where, Aunt Joanne!?" Andrea demanded. "What happened? Where is Uncle Charles??"

Her aunt managed to speak. "There is a dry well on the side of the house. It's been boarded up for ages. Charles knew it was there, yet somehow he fell into it. Tom, Jesse's dad, found him this morning. He's badly injured. The ambulance is here, and we are taking him to the hospital in the city. I have to go right now."

Andrea could barely breathe. "I'll go with you."

"No, honey, you can't. Please just stay here in the house, where you're safe. I'm sorry to leave you like this, but there's no time. Tom will be in the bunkhouse. I'll call you as soon as I can." Aunt Joanne whirled and raced from the room.

Andrea watched from the window as the ambulance pulled away. As soon as she was alone she ran to the studio. The painted face of Don Hidalgo was twisted into a hideous grin. She stared at it in terror. Right before her eyes it seemed to shift its gaze to her in triumph.

Andrea thought about Uncle Charles, fighting for his life. "You haven't won!" she yelled at the painting. "I'll find a way to stop you."

For the next few hours she combed through the books in Uncle Charles's library. She found one on the history of the valley. It told of Ramon Hidalgo's many crimes. There was another book, too—an old, leatherbound volume about witchcraft and sorcery. Andrea read the fading print on its yellowed pages and slowly hatched a plan.

She brought a can of gasoline from the barn and carried it to the studio. Her parents had taught her the dangers of handling such things, but she felt it was her only choice. She struggled to get the huge painting from the wall and dragged it to the oversized fireplace. All the while she talked to the painting. "I'm going to stop you once and for all," she said. "Now all I have to do is wait just a little longer."

When the afternoon had begun to deepen into twilight, Jesse knocked at the door. "I thought you might like some company," he said. "Have you heard any news?"

"Not yet," Andrea said. Then she whispered, "But I'm glad you're here. I need your help." She took Jesse by the hand and, telling him what she had learned about the painting, she led him toward the studio. "As long as Don Hidalgo has a link to the living world, he can hurt us. We have to destroy the painting after nightfall. That is when the painting can change and is most vulnerable."

Jesse never even questioned her. Andrea opened the door to her aunt's studio, and together they stepped inside.

"Jesse!" Andrea almost screamed. "Look, he's not there!"

Moonlight streaming in from the glass doors of the veranda revealed an empty space in the center of the painting. As the children watched, a shadow fell across the canvas. Slowly, they both turned to see the figure of Don Hidalgo standing in the doorway behind them. His eyes were seething with hatred as he slowly spoke. "So, you thought you would end my time here on earth. You stupid mortals— you do not have any idea of the depth of my power."

"But I do," Andrea answered bravely. "Without the painting you are nothing." She held up a package of matches in her trembling hand.

The hideous creature threw back his head and laughed. Then he scowled wickedly at the matches, and the entire pack suddenly flared in Andrea's hand.

She screamed and dropped the burning pack, then lunged for the can of gasoline by the door. But Don Hidalgo turned his gaze to it and the can exploded into bits. Then he lifted his hand, and somehow Andrea went slamming into a wall. Breathless, she sank to the floor.

Jesse charged across the room at the fiendish phantom, but it stopped him in his tracks. Don Hidalgo's unblinking eyes held Jesse's much the way the eyes of a snake hold the gaze of its victim. Don Hidalgo reached out and wrapped his icy fingers around the boy's throat and squeezed. Darkness flowed over Jesse in waves, and he could see the face of one of the figures in the painting taking on his own features.

"NOOOOOOOOOOO!" Andrea screamed, struggling to her feet. She grabbed a bottle of fluid from her aunt's supply table and threw it at the ghastly creature. The bottle missed him, but hit the painting and shattered, drenching the canvas with a clear, smelly fluid. Don Hidalgo stared at the painting in disbelief as the colors began to run together. His grip weakened, and Jesse felt air rush back into his lungs.

Andrea raced to her friend's side as the strong smell of turpentine filled the room. "Are you all right?" she gasped. But Jesse motioned toward Don Hidalgo. He was running his fingers through the oozing colors as if he were trying to put them back where they belonged. Then his body began to sag. His entire face was hanging in dripping streams of flesh. Opening his formless mouth one last time, he howled weakly in defeat. Then everything was silent.

"Come on," Andrea said, helping Jesse to his feet. "Let's call the hospital. I have a feeling that Uncle Charles is going to be all right now."

For a moment, all was still. A shaft of silvery moonlight reached the puddle on the floor, and slowly the colors began to swirl. Then gradually, deliberately, they flowed across the empty canvas in bold strokes, and a new portrait began to take shape . . . a new portrait of evil.

⟫◆⟪

All the Time in the World

he *Tyrannosaurus rex* was definitely the most ferocious of the meat-eaters. It was huge!" Kara spread her arms as wide as she could to make her point.

David shook his head. "Just because a dinosaur was the biggest of its kind doesn't mean it was the meanest."

The two friends were sitting cross-legged in David's room. Dinosaurs and ancient mammals of various types glowered down at them from posters on the walls. One very large book was open on the floor between them. David had borrowed it from his next-door neighbor, Alden. "Pound for pound," David said firmly, "some prehistoric mammals were a *lot* tougher than dinosaurs. Alden told me."

Like David, Alden loved prehistoric creatures. He was a grown-up, but he didn't really act like one. During the day he drove a delivery truck. At night he stayed up until all hours working on weird inventions in his basement.

Kara leaned over David and peered into the book. "Okay, which ones were tougher than dinosaurs?"

David pointed to a picture of a heavy-fanged, catlike beast, but he was interrupted by a knock. His father opened the door and leaned in.

"David, your mother asked you almost an hour ago to go next door and clean up the mess in Alden's driveway. I suggest you take care of it now before it gets dark."

"Aw, Dad. I didn't make the mess. Why don't we just let Alden clean it up himself?"

"Because it was your dog that tipped over his trash can," David's mom said as she stepped into the room. "Besides, Alden isn't there. I went over the day before yesterday to give him a package that had been delivered here by mistake, but he didn't answer the door. He wasn't there this morning either. Maybe he's away on a trip and forgot to mention that he was leaving. You know how forgetful he can be."

"C'mon, David. I'll help you," Kara offered.

The two children collected a broom and dustpan, then went outside and surveyed the mess. "What is all this junk?" Kara asked. The driveway was strewn with bits and pieces of cable, wire, graph paper and what looked like tiny electrical parts that had been fried to a crisp.

"Alden is working on a new project. He's been fooling with it for a couple of months," David said, picking up a handful of papers and dumping them into the trash. "Usually he likes to show me his inventions, but this time he's being real secretive about it. I haven't seen him at all in more than a week. Maybe Mom's right. Maybe he's on a trip."

"Do you think something's wrong?" Kara asked.

David furrowed his brow. "I'm going to see if his car is here. I'll be right back."

A moment later David returned. "Alden's car is here all right. Maybe we should take a look inside the house. Maybe he's sick or something."

The kids went to the front door and rang the bell. There was no answer. They tried the back door too, then David noticed that the window next to the door was open slightly. He slipped his fingers under the windowsill, pushed it all the way up and climbed inside.

Kara hesitated. "I don't know if we should do this."

"We're not going to do anything wrong. We're just checking to see if Alden is inside," David said, a little annoyed. "Maybe he fell down the stairs and needs help. If we save him, we'll be heroes."

The idea of being a hero seemed like a good one, so Kara hoisted herself up over the windowsill and into the kitchen. "PE-YEW!" she wrinkled up her nose in disgust.

The place was deserted. Dirty dishes were in the sink, and a carton of milk had been left out on the counter. "This place is kind of spooky," Kara whispered. "Let's hurry up. I'll look in here," she said stepping into the living room.

Suddenly a low growl issued from somewhere in the shadows. Kara froze. A deep voice boomed out, "Stay right where you are. I've got you covered!"

"Don't shoot!" Kara pleaded.

David just laughed. "Oh, I forgot." He walked into the living room and flipped a switch on a tape player on a bookshelf. "Look," he said, pointing to a wire that ran from under the carpet where Kara was standing. "It's Alden's version of a burglar alarm."

Within minutes the children had checked the upper levels of the house, but Alden was nowhere to be found. The last place to check was the workshop in the basement.

"Wow!" Kara said as they started down the basement stairs. A counter and shelves ran around the entire room and everything was cluttered with machines, tools and parts. "This place is great! Look at this stuff. What does it all do?"

"Most of it doesn't do anything. Alden isn't a very good inventor," David explained. "Hey, that's new." He pointed toward a large object in the center of the room. It looked like four round platforms piled on top of one another, creating a series of steps. A post about three feet high was in the center. There were lights all around the post, and it was topped with what looked like a small television screen.

The kids climbed up onto the upper platform and studied the switches and dials. "It must be some sort of vehicle," David guessed. "Let's find out!" He flicked one of the switches.

"Yeah!" Kara grinned and flicked a few more switches.

All at once a purple light came on around the rim of the bottom step and bathed the entire floor in lavender.

"Awesome!" Kara flicked another switch and wide, green beams of light shot out from the second platform. Then a low humming sound came from the post. Another switch sent streams of blue light in every direction from the third platform. Finally, David touched the uppermost switch. Red beams from the fourth and final platform flowed upward, and the children were enclosed in a curtain of ruby-colored light. The post on the screen whirred to life. It was a digital counter of some kind.

Kara's face whitened as the machine began to vibrate. "David, I don't think I like this. Shut it off!"

David pushed at the switches, but they were all locked into position. "I don't know how!" he shouted. The counter continued to whirl, and the humming sound grew louder.

"I thought you knew all about this stuff. What if this is a bomb? Do something!" Kara yelled at the top of her lungs.

Abruptly, everything became quiet. The red, blue, and green lights turned off, leaving the room glowing silently in an eerie lavender light. The children looked around. Aside from the light, everything looked the same—except the digital counter on the screen. It read 1,000,000.

"It turned itself off," David said. "I guess everything is okay. Maybe we should . . . " But he was interrupted by a loud, fierce roar, followed by what sounded like heavy footsteps coming from outside.

"What was that?" Kara's voice was shaky.

David tried to be calm. "It's probably another one of Alden's stupid burglar alarms. Let's go see."

Kara shook her head. "Uh-uh—I don't think so."

"C'mon, we can't stay down here. Besides, it's getting really hot and stuffy. I need some air."

Reluctantly, Kara followed her friend up the basement stairs. At the top, David gripped the doorknob. It was warm to the touch. David turned it and slowly opened the door.

A wispy tendril of fog snaked into the room. The two youngsters stood in the doorway, their mouths wide open. The house, the neighborhood, everything they knew was gone. Instead, they seemed to be on some sort of highland. To their right the land sloped down sharply, flattened, and stretched into a barren plain all the way to the horizon.

"Where are we?" Kara whispered.

David looked closely at the trees and plants crowded outside of the door. "From the looks of these plants, I think the question should be, *when* are we? This looks an awful lot like a kind of place that would have existed a couple of million years ago." He was finding it hard to breathe. "Wait a minute. Maybe this isn't really happening. Maybe we're just imagining it. The machine probably gives off some kind of gas that makes you *think* you're somewhere else. It's possible that if we just step out of the room and take a few deep breaths, everything will be the way it was."

"Do you really think so?" Kara asked.

"Do you have a better idea?"

The two moved cautiously through the doorway and out a few feet into the strange forest. Behind them the door was a glowing purple blur.

"Breathe in deeply," David instructed. They each took several lungfuls of air.

"I think it's working!" Kara cried out. "The trees are starting to quiver. Look!"

All at once a large, low branch was flung to one side and they were staring into a huge, bearlike face. The beast reared up, towering at least fifteen feet tall. Each of its massive paws sported long, sharp claws that were curved like scythes. The animal took a heavy step forward, placing its enormous body between the children and the door.

David gasped. "It's a *Megatherium*!"

Kara was trembling all over. She spoke in a low undertone. "What does that mean?"

"It won't hurt us. It's a plant-eater."

"Does it know that?" Kara moaned, backing away.

In a rapid move, it swiped at them with a giant paw. Kara took another backward step and slid down the side of the embankment in an avalanche of loose rock. "David!" she screamed. He raced after her, gripping her by the arm before she reached the edge of the drop-off.

"C'mon," he panted, helping her to her feet. "We've got to get back to the . . ." But he didn't finish. His eyes were wide with fear. Their escape was blocked by something deadly.

Crouched on a rock above them was what looked like a lion, except that its lips were drawn back in a snarl that revealed an arsenal of teeth unlike any lion of the modern world. Protruding from its upper jaw were a pair of glistening fangs as long as daggers.

David tried to speak. "Kara," he murmured hoarsely, "we'll have to make a run for the forest."

But the creature seemed to second-guess the two children and lunged for them just as they made their break for the shelter of the undergrowth. With the beast on her heels, Kara started to clamber up into the limbs of a tall tree.

"No!" David screamed. "It can reach you there. We've got to find a place to hide that is too small for it to get into. There!" He pointed to an outcrop of rock about fifty yards away. They reached it in seconds and scrambled in among the boulders.

"I don't think it followed us up here," David gasped.

"Tell me I'm crazy," Kara groaned, "but wasn't that one of those things in the book we were looking at?"

"Yeah . . . a saber-toothed cat, a *Smilodon*," David wheezed. He wiped the sweat from his eyes and leaned out from their hiding place to survey the surroundings. "I think it's gone, so we can . . . AAAAAAHHHHH!"

Without warning, a figure leaped out from behind another boulder and pulled David to the ground. He struggled out from underneath the weight, grabbed a small rock and lifted it to strike the attacker.

"No!" Kara yelled. "It's a person!"

David stopped and stared at the figure on the ground. It was Alden! He was badly battered and bruised, and he was very pale. His left arm hung limply at his side at an odd angle.

"Alden?" David gasped. "Alden, what . . . ?" But before the man could speak, they heard a throaty snarl.

David and Kara pulled Alden further into the safety of the rocks and leaned him against a boulder. He looked pretty bad, but he tried to smile.

"David, Kara—am I glad to see you! You didn't happen to bring anything to eat, did you?"

David fished into his jacket pocket and pulled out a squashed candy bar. He unwrapped it and put it in Alden's right hand. Alden held it tightly, but he didn't attempt to take a bite. David noticed that several of his teeth were gone.

"How did you figure out where I was? Who figured out how to use the machine? Who else is with you?" the badly injured man asked in short, breathy gasps.

"Nobody's with us," David answered. "We were looking for you, and we saw the machine in the basement. We just wanted to see what it did. Then, suddenly, we ended up here."

Alden groaned. "The machine must still be preset for the Pleistocene epoch. I was testing it," he said, wincing in pain. "The only way back is through the door. Each time the passage is opened, it remains open for one hour unless you close it down from the machine. If you don't get back through it, you won't survive long in this time period." As if to make the point, something in the forest growled menacingly.

"Okay," David said bravely. "The door isn't very far. We can carry you between us. We'll make it."

Alden shook his head. "You won't get back unless you can run. There are things in the forest. . . ." He touched the terrible gouges in his arm. "They come out of nowhere."

"We know," Kara said. "We ran into a *Smilodon*. That's how we got this far."

Alden curled one side of his mouth into a bitter grin. "It isn't one cat you have to worry about. You could probably outrun him and hide. But the dire wolves—they're bigger and faster, and they work together in packs. Worst of it is, they're smart. They're responsible for what happened to me." Weakly, he held up his torn arm, then let it drop. "The pack is still out there. It's too late for me, kids. I'm out of time." Alden drew in a shallow breath. "You go on alone. . . . It's the only way." David started to protest, but Alden cut him off. "There's no more time to discuss it. Now go!"

David touched Alden's shoulder, then looked at his watch. "We have fifteen minutes, Kara. Let's go for it."

Kara and David moved as fast as they could through the

undergrowth. Soon they could see the purplish glow of the door. When they were only a few yards away, David heard a rustling behind them. Then his eye caught sight of a dark shadow, then another, moving among the trees.

"It's the dire wolves. They're surrounding us!" he yelled.

The kids took off as fast as they could, crashing through the leaves and twigs. Kara tripped, and as she regained her footing, she looked over her shoulder. Four vicious-looking animals were racing toward them. They all had savage claws, and their dripping jaws were lined with flesh-ripping teeth. One of the wolves was close enough to make a try for its prey. Snarling, it leaped into the air, snapping its jaws. Kara

thought her heart would burst, but she made a final effort and vaulted forward. She crashed into David, and they both tumbled through the doorway.

For a moment the terrified children stayed perfectly still at the bottom of the stairs. Finally Kara whispered, "I think we made it. Are you okay?"

David nodded. At the top of the stairs, the purple glow faded. David looked at his watch. "We just made it. Let's reset the machine and go home."

Moments later Kara and David slipped back out of Alden's kitchen window. "Poor Alden," Kara murmured. "I wish we could have helped him. Thank goodness it's over."

David suddenly turned back to the gate. "It isn't over! When we came through the time passage we opened it for another hour. We have to go back down and close the channel from the machine. Something might be able to get through!"

The kids raced back through the garden and in through the kitchen window. As they stepped into the darkened living room they heard a low growl.

"It's just Alden's stupid tape," David said. "Come on."

But in the darkness, they didn't see the two massive creatures crouching by the basement stairs . . . two fellow time travelers, with razor-sharp teeth.

Household Help

 hate homework, and I hate softball and I hate school!" Hannah threw her books on the kitchen counter and slumped into a chair at the table. Claudine, the housekeeper, was busy making dinner, and the noise made her jump. Hannah's mom looked up from her own books spread out across the tabletop. She was studying for a night class she was taking at the community college.

"I know how you feel, honey," she said. "Sometimes it seems like there is so much to learn that you'll never get done. But you have to keep trying. Is there anything I can do?"

Hannah grunted. "Not unless you can pitch and hit. I wish I were like Stephanie Lake. She's the best pitcher the team has ever had. And she can hit, too." Hannah frowned. "But then *she* doesn't have to do a makeup report for science class. She doesn't have to work hard at anything!"

"I'm sure that isn't true," Hannah's mom said. "But you'll never get anywhere feeling sorry for yourself. You have to take control of things." She stood up and gathered together a few papers. "Look, I have a test tonight, and I have to get ready for class. Tomorrow is Saturday. Maybe after the game I can help you with that science report, okay? And good luck with your game. I know you'll do great." She kissed her daughter on the forehead, then left.

Claudine brought Hannah a glass of milk. "This will keep the hunger away until dinner," she said, smiling. Claudine was a pleasant, grandmotherly woman. She had come to work for the family when Hannah's mom had started school three months ago, and she took her job very seriously.

"Thanks, Claudine," Hannah said, putting down the empty glass. "You always seem to know exactly what I want."

Claudine smiled. "I take pride in doing my job well. While I am working for a family, I am very loyal to them, and I believe it is my duty to do everything in my power to take care of them." She emphasized the word *power*.

"What do you mean?" Hannah asked.

The housekeeper glanced toward the door and lowered her voice. "I don't want to see you unhappy. If you are, that means I am not doing my job well. It is important to me that you get what you want. Perhaps I could help you with your softball. You see, I have these special . . . talents."

Hannah was a little confused. "You play softball?"

Claudine laughed. It was a twittering sound that made

98

Hannah uneasy. "Oh, no. But I can help you, anyway. Tonight, when your momma is gone, I will show you."

· · · · · · · · · ·

After dinner, Hannah's mother left for school. Claudine busied herself with the dishes. Hannah thought about what the housekeeper had said earlier about helping her, but she dismissed it. She was working on her report when Claudine knocked at the door of her room.

"I am ready," she announced. Out of curiosity, Hannah followed her to the family room.

"What's going on?" the girl asked. There were candles lit on every table, and the room smelled all perfumy.

"Step into the center of the room and sit down," Claudine commanded.

"This is really weird," Hannah said, "and it smells funny in here." Still, she did as the woman instructed.

While Hannah sat on the floor, the housekeeper walked around her chanting. Finally, she took an object from her apron pocket. It was a small odd-shaped root, and one end had a small ring attached to it. The root was strung on a thin cord that Claudine slipped over Hannah's head.

"You must wear this at all times," she informed the girl. "Never let anyone, not even me, take it from you."

But Hannah couldn't bear the idea of sleeping with the ugly thing on, so she didn't follow the instructions exactly. When she was getting ready for bed, she slipped the root off and put it on her dresser. In the morning she saw the root

lying there. Feeling a little foolish, she slipped the cord over her head and tucked the unsightly thing under her shirt.

By the time she got to the park, Hannah had forgotten the silly ritual that Claudine had performed the night before—that is, until she stood at home plate facing a pitcher, with two of her teammates on base. As the softball left the pitcher's hand, Hannah felt the root wriggle slightly against her chest. The movement scared her, and she jerked the bat. It came in contact with the softball with a resounding crack, and the ball sailed over the fence! In the stands, her classmates and their parents were wild with excitement.

After the game, many people came up to congratulate Hannah on making the winning hit. She was really enjoying the glory when Stephanie Lake walked up to her.

"Good going, Hannah," Stephanie said. "You couldn't have picked a better time to get such a lucky hit."

Hannah scowled. Why did Stephanie have to put it that way? It spoiled everything.

• • • • • • • • • •

That night after dinner, while her mom was studying, Hannah slipped into the kitchen to talk to Claudine. The woman smiled broadly at her as she entered the room. "See, my child? I told you I could help."

"Yes," Hannah agreed. "You were right. When you said it was your duty to take care of us, you really meant it."

"Of course," the old woman said.

"Good." Hannah grinned. "Because now I have another problem."

"Oh?" Claudine said warily. "And what is that?"

"It's no good making the winning hit if people think it was just luck. I want to be good at things all the time. I especially want to do things better than Stephanie Lake."

Claudine raised an eyebrow and looked at Hannah. "Just because a single piece of pie gives you happiness, it doesn't mean that you will be any happier having the entire pie. The result might not be what you expect."

"You said that it was your job to take care of your family," Hannah said. "Well, being better than Stephanie Lake is what I want. In fact, I want to make a fool out of her in front of everybody! It's your job to see that I get what I want. Now, when do we do that circle thing?"

Claudine stared at her for a moment. "That won't be necessary," she said finally. "I will be right back." A moment later she returned with a tiny vial of liquid. "Just rub this into the root," she instructed. "You will get what you want."

• • • • • • • • • •

As Claudine had promised, Hannah excelled in everything she tried at softball practice that Monday. The coach even let her pitch, and she struck out every batter. In fact, the coach promised that if she kept playing so well she could pitch in the game on Saturday. When Stephanie stepped up to bat, Hannah made sure that she didn't get a hit. She threw the ball hard and struck Stephanie in the arm.

"You did that on purpose!" Stephanie wailed. A large red welt was forming where the ball had walloped her.

"C'mon, Stephanie," Hannah smirked. "Why would I do that? It was an accident. You're just upset because the coach let me pitch." Hannah could see that Stephanie was trying to hold back tears. "Hey, look at this," Hannah said aloud. "Just because she doesn't get her own way, Stephanie's gonna start crying!" A couple of the other kids laughed. It was too much for Stephanie. She launched herself at Hannah.

"That's enough!" the coach shouted, breaking up the fight. "You're both sitting out Saturday's game."

"Are you satisfied, jerk?" Stephanie muttered.

Hannah set her mouth in a hard line and glared at Stephanie as she walked away.

· · · · · · · · · ·

Hannah didn't wait until after dinner to corner Claudine. She went straight home and marched into the kitchen. "Claudine!" she said angrily. "I need you to really fix somebody!"

"Child," the old woman said, looking deep into Hannah's eyes. "Forget your anger and let it go."

"You wouldn't say that if you knew what happened today," Hannah declared.

"I know more than you might expect," Claudine answered solemnly. "And I know that a trap set for prey can close just as easily on the hunter."

"I don't want to listen to any mumbo-jumbo. You swore to take care of me, and I want to get even with Stephanie

Lake. Can you really make her suffer?"

"I do not have control over what takes place. I simply do my part to guide your own energies. It comes from you."

"Whatever," Hannah grumbled. "Just take care of it."

Claudine gazed at her sadly. "Bring me the root."

When the ritual was finished, Hannah took back the root and placed it on her dresser where she kept it at night. She still couldn't bear the thought of sleeping with it around her neck, even though Claudine had warned her to do so.

· · · · · · · · · ·

The minute she got to school the next morning, Hannah could tell that something was wrong. She noticed that Stephanie wasn't there. As soon as everyone was seated, the teacher announced that something terrible had happened. Stephanie's mother had been involved in a serious automobile accident, and Stephanie and her family were at the hospital. The teacher said that Mrs. Lake would be all right, and that Stephanie would be in school the next day.

For a moment, Hannah felt a pang of guilt. She hadn't meant for something like this to happen. "It'll be okay," she told herself. "Mrs. Poole said she would be all right."

· · · · · · · · · ·

When she got home, Hannah avoided going into the kitchen to see Claudine. She went straight to her room.

The next morning, she woke up late. She dressed quickly and went to the dresser to get the root. It was gone.

"Mom!" she called out. "Did you take anything from my dresser?"

"No," her mom called back. "Is it important?"

Hannah hesitated. How could she explain what it was? "It was nothing," she told her mom before leaving the house for school. She would talk to the housekeeper when she got home.

· · · · · · · · · ·

At school, Hannah saw that Stephanie was back.

"I'm sorry about your mom," Hannah said sincerely as she passed the other girl's desk. But Stephanie said nothing. She just glared up at Hannah.

When it was time to read their reports, Hannah volunteered to do hers first. As she walked to the front of the class, she tripped over a book and landed flat in the aisle. Her classmates burst into laughter. Hannah's face burned red with embarrassment. When she looked up, Stephanie was crouched next to her, stone-faced, helping to pick up the scattered pages of Hannah's report. Then, as she handed the papers to Hannah, Stephanie whispered, "This is only the beginning." She leaned forward to stand up, and Hannah saw a carved root on a cord slip out from under her sweater.

"Hey, that's mine," Hannah snarled.

"Not anymore," Stephanie sneered.

After school Hannah raced home from the bus stop. She

burst through the front door yelling, "Claudine! Claudine!" When she bounded into the kitchen, she saw her mother at the sink, peeling vegetables for dinner.

"Whoa! What's all the fuss?" her mom asked.

Hannah was out of breath. "Mom, it's important," she gasped. "I have to speak to Claudine."

"Well you can't," her mom informed her. "She isn't here."

"Isn't h . . . where is she?" Hannah demanded.

Her mother dried her hands on a towel and looked quizzically at her daughter. "I was thinking of letting her go because I will only have one class next semester. Then I heard what happened to poor Mrs. Lake. She's going to need help now for a long time, so I recommended Claudine. She left last night. I didn't have time to tell you. But it worked out just perfectly. Now Mrs. Lake has help, and Claudine has a new family to take care of."

———⟫◆⟪———

The Snow Cave

elinda's dad pulled the car into the parking space in front of the general store.

"Okay, honey," he said. "I'm going to get some supplies and order the wood we need for the whole two weeks we'll be in the cabin. They're predicting snow and we'll appreciate a nice warm fire."

"Sounds great, Dad," she agreed. "Can I take a walk with Shiloh?"

"Sure, but don't go far. And zip up your jacket," he called after her. "It's getting pretty cold."

Belinda clipped Shiloh's leash to his collar and opened the car door. The excited husky bounded out and stood beside the truck, his tail wagging. Together, Belinda and Shiloh strolled along the sidewalk, looking in shop windows. When they returned, two gray-haired men were sitting on wooden chairs outside the general store.

"That's a fine animal," one of the men said. Shiloh took a liking to the man right away and waited to be petted. "Are you the young lady whose folks rented the Rogers's cabin?"

"Yes, sir," she answered. "If there's enough snow, my dad is going to teach me to ski."

"If there is *too* much," the second man said seriously, "you could get more than you bargained for."

"I beg your pardon?" Belinda tilted her head in question.

"Don't mind old Frank," the first man, whose name was Willis, advised. "He's just afraid of the snowman."

Belinda laughed. "Afraid of a snowman?"

The smile disappeared from Willis's face. "We're not talking about a ball of snow with a carrot nose and a top hat. Have you ever heard of the yeti?"

Belinda nodded. "They're huge apelike creatures in the mountains in Asia. But it's only a legend."

Willis leaned back in his chair. "According to a local Indian legend, something like the yeti once lived in these mountains. Maybe it still does." The man's eyes twinkled. "There's a chain of underground caves around here, with several different openings to the surface. Nobody knows just how far they go back, or what might be living in them."

Belinda was fascinated. "If there are snow creatures here, why hasn't anyone seen them?"

Frank took a long drag on his pipe and let the smoke slowly curl from his lips. "Maybe some people did. Back in

'39, when we were kids, we used to play up at that ridge where the Rogers's cabin stands now. It was a good hill for sledding. One weekend there was a real heavy snowfall. All we wanted was to have fun." His voice faltered and his face clouded over, as if the memory of that weekend was painful.

"One of our group," said Willis, picking up the story, "was a boy named Wally. Somehow, Wally got lost . . . just disappeared. Some folks figured they'd find the body in spring, but they never did. All we ever found was one of his red mittens and his broken sled, with deep scratches in it . . . like claw marks." Willis glanced at Frank. "There are a few who think a yeti got him. According to the legend, they come to the surface to hunt when there's a lot of snow."

"And isn't it strange," Frank added, "that every time we have a major snowfall some hiker or skier suddenly disappears? No body . . . no nothing."

"Has anyone disappeared lately?" Belinda asked.

"No, but we haven't had much snow for eight years."

The door to the general store swung open and Belinda's dad stepped out with two large grocery bags. He placed them in the trunk of the car and joined Belinda and the men. "Might one of you fellas be Willis?" he asked.

Willis nodded. "That's me."

"I'm Joe McGowan," Belinda's dad said, smiling. "They told me inside to check with you about getting the wood delivered to the cabin."

"Sure, no problem," Willis answered. "Frank and I will get it loaded in the truck and I'll bring it up shortly."

"That'll be fine," Mr. McGowan said, then turned to Belinda. "Come on, honey. We're all set. If we don't get back to the cabin soon your mom will start to get worried."

As they got into the van, it began to snow. Belinda told her dad about the legend.

He laughed. "Well, I can't say that I believe in snow monsters, but there is a good point to the story. These woods *can* be dangerous, and people can easily get lost."

Belinda buried her fingers in Shiloh's thick coat. "I don't have to worry as long as Shiloh's with me," she said. "Isn't that right, boy?" Shiloh answered by licking her ear.

It wasn't a long drive, but by the time they got to the cabin the snow was piling up. Within an hour Willis arrived with the firewood, and Belinda and her dad helped him to unload it. Belinda's mom made them all a hot cup of cocoa, which they drank in the living room in front of a warm fire.

After a while, Willis set down his cup. "I don't mean to rush off," he said, as he pulled on his jacket, "but it looks like the weather's getting worse. I think I'd best get back to town. We haven't had this much snow in a long time."

Belinda glanced out the window at the darkening landscape. As if he knew what she was thinking, Willis laughed. "Don't be concerned, little lady. The storm will blow over by tomorrow." He trudged out into the snow, then stopped and called back over his shoulder. "If you folks need anything, just call down to the general store."

• • • • • • • • • •

Willis was wrong. It snowed the whole night and through the next day and night, too. The report on the radio said that it was the most snow that had fallen in thirty years.

The following day the clouds cleared. The air was cold and crisp, and huge snowdrifts glistened in the winter sunshine. Belinda was too excited to think about snow monsters. Her dad had rented three large innertubes that were perfect for sliding downhill. Belinda dressed warmly. Her parents had taught her to respect nature and prepare for anything, so she also packed a few supplies in a fannypack.

It took some time for the family to work their way up through the soft snow to the top of the ridge behind the cabin, but it was worth it. There was a long, wide clearing on the hill, with dense forest on each side. Soon Belinda and her parents were taking turns whizzing down the open patch of hillside in their rubber tubes, then scrambling back up again for another ride. Each time Belinda swooshed downward, Shiloh raced along behind. He barked and tumbled in the snow, seeming to really enjoy the game.

"Whew!" Belinda's mom exclaimed as they scrunched up the hill together. "I think I've had enough."

"Oh, Mom—just one more ride?" Belinda begged. "Why don't we all race to the bottom of the hill?"

"Okay!" her dad said. "Last one to the bottom is a rotten egg!" He took off. Laughing, Belinda and her mom each belly flopped onto their tubes and raced after him.

Belinda was a little behind when her tube hit a patch of icy snow and veered off to the right. She tried to correct the turn, but she was going too fast. The tube sped in among the trees and headed for a huge pine. Belinda tumbled off the tube and rolled into a big drift of snow. Helpless, she slid downward, picking up speed toward a wide, flat rock that stuck up out of a drift. She curled in her legs and covered her head with her arms, expecting to crash. But instead of hitting the rock she slid through a small opening beneath it. She slid further into the darkness, then felt herself tumble over a ledge and fall about five feet straight down. Screaming into the nothingness, Belinda finally came to an abrupt stop on cold, hard ground. Then everything went black.

At first, when she came to, Belinda thought that she had been dreaming. But as soon as she moved, she knew it was all real. Nothing seemed to be broken, but she was sore all over. If it hadn't been for her layers of padded winter clothing, she would surely have been seriously hurt by the fall. She reached under her jacket and was relieved to find that the fannypack was still strapped to her waist. Fumbling a little in the inky blackness, she pulled out her small flashlight, clicked it on and surveyed her surroundings.

"Wow," she said aloud to herself. "What is this place?" The beam of light revealed a large cave with several tunnels leading from it. She moved the light up and saw an opening above her and realized she had fallen through it. Slowly, she stood up and rubbed her sore legs. The opening was just a little out of reach. She looked around to see if there was anything to stand on. The cave was empty.

"HELLO!" she called out. "HELLO! I'm down here. Can anybody hear me?" There was no answer. How long had she been down here? She realized that her parents must be searching for her, but they probably had not seen her careen off into the forest. How would they find her?

"There must be another way out," she murmured, remembering what Willis had said about the caves and how there were several openings to the surface. She tried not to think about the other things he had told her.

Taking a deep breath, Belinda chose one of the tunnels and entered it. In some places she had to duck way down and crawl. She had the feeling that she was heading further down, but where else could she go? She had to try it.

Finally, the passage opened up into another wide cavern. Belinda shone the flashlight around and noted that there were other tunnels. Then her foot kicked something. She turned the beam on it and screamed at the empty eye sockets staring blindly up at her. It was a human skull. In horror, Belinda moved the flashlight beam a little further and saw that the skull was attached to other bones that had once been the body of a child. And worst of all, the skeleton had a single red mitten on one hand!

"Wally!" she cried, not hearing the muffled footsteps slipping up behind her in the dark. Then, all at once, she felt a presence. Slowly she turned and saw a horrible monster in the glare of her flashlight. It was a huge beast covered with stiff, white fur. It had enormous, bloodshot eyes and a snarling mouth full of sharp, yellow fangs. Roaring in anger, the creature slashed at Belinda with its thick, bearlike claws.

She ducked the blow and dashed for another tunnel. Her heart pounding, she sprinted along the twisting passage and, bursting into an open space, saw the very same skeleton she had seen before. "The tunnels must be interconnected," she whispered frantically. "I'm going in circles!"

Although she had no idea where the beast might be, Belinda tried another entrance and stumbled along, drawing in the stale air in ragged gasps. After what seemed like ages,

she found herself once again in the same horrible chamber. Without hesitating, she dashed into another tunnel.

This time she seemed to be climbing, perhaps toward the surface! The thought gave her courage and she ran faster. Then, suddenly, she stumbled. Grabbing an outcrop of rock, she managed to stop her fall. She shone her flashlight ahead and saw that she was actually at the rim of some sort of ledge. One side of the tunnel dropped away into a deep, wide crevasse. As she tried to see how far along the path the crevasse ran, her flashlight dimmed and slowly faded out.

Belinda's heart sank. Now she was completely enveloped in darkness. The hairs stood up on the back of

her neck as she heard the echoing sound of a low snarl. Where was it coming from? How close was it? She set her jaw in determination. She was not going to just sit and wait for the snow monster to find her. Instead, she dropped to her knees and carefully felt her way along the path. "I *will* get out," she said to herself. To keep her spirits up, she thought of Shiloh. For a moment, she smiled as she remembered his excited bark. It seemed that she could actually hear it.

"Wait a minute!" Belinda said aloud as she straightened up. "I *do* hear it." She strained her ears. "Shiloh?"

Now she could hear voices, too . . . human voices.

"Belinda!" her dad called.

"DAD! I'm over here," she cried. Slowly, the tunnel brightened. A moment later, her father and another man turned a corner with Shiloh leading them.

"DAD!!" Belinda jumped to her feet and ran toward them. But with a bloodcurdling snarl, the snow monster leaped from a side tunnel. Inches away from her, it raised its claws, then suddenly cried out in agony. Shiloh had raced ahead and sunk his teeth into the beast's leg.

The hideous monster twisted clumsily to strike at the dog, but Shiloh held on as the savage snow creature toppled and fell, howling into the crevasse. "Shiloh! Let go!" Belinda screamed as she threw herself forward and grabbed Shiloh to stop him from falling with the monster.

Belinda's dad reached them and scooped her up in his arms. "It's okay, baby," he said comfortingly. "We're getting you out of here."

A little later, Belinda awoke in her own bed. Her mother was sitting at her side and Shiloh was stretched out on the floor chewing on a big, meaty bone.

"Mom?" Belinda sat up. "Was it a dream?"

"No, honey," her mother said, hugging her tightly.

"How did you find me?"

Belinda's mother smiled down at the husky at her feet. "Shiloh led us to the spot where you had disappeared. It was too small for us to get through, so we had to get help. Once we were able to widen the opening, Shiloh led the rescue party to you. Many townspeople came to help."

There was a knock at the door, and Willis poked his head inside. "I came to see if you were all right," he said gently.

"I'm fine now," Belinda said, "Is the monster dead?"

"We can only hope so," Willis answered. He stood near the window, watching the first flakes of a new snowstorm.

Shiloh lifted his head and turned his gaze to the window, too. Then he drew back his lip slightly to show his front fangs, and a low growl rumbled in his throat.

"It's okay, boy," Belinda soothed.

But then, of course, Belinda couldn't pick up the scent of the creature that stood at the edge of the woods, staring toward the cabin with enormous, bloodshot eyes.

———⟫◆⟪———

The Fabulous Flyers

nd why can't I have them?" Kevin crossed his arms and scowled at his mother.

"We can't afford them," she answered wearily. "You know I get you what I can. Besides, you already have sneakers."

"But I don't have Fabulous Flyers," Kevin whined. "All the coolest kids have them."

"You could save up for them," his mom suggested.

"It would take me forever." Kevin pouted. "You got Ellen a new doll."

"It was your sister's birthday, Kevin." His mom was starting to get angry. "Your own birthday is coming up. We'll see about it then. Now, the subject is closed."

"My birthday isn't for three months," Kevin said, stamping his foot like a three-year-old.

His mother glared at him. "The subject is closed."

In a huff, Kevin picked up his books and stormed out of the kitchen. His mother just didn't understand. Some things—how you walked and talked, and what clothes you wore—were really important. Those were the things that made you cool and popular. And being popular was more important to Kevin than anything.

As he started to push open the front door, Kevin noticed his sister's new doll on the couch. "Stupid thing," he muttered to himself. He picked up the doll and twisted its head until he heard a snapping sound and the head hung loosely from the doll's neck. Kevin smiled and threw the ruined toy on the floor. Breaking it made him feel a little better.

•••••••••••

At school Kevin saw that even the school nerd, Franco Roberts, was wearing a new pair of Fabulous Flyers. Now Kevin really *was* the only sixth grader without them. By the time his best friend, Walter, flopped down in the seat next to him at lunch, Kevin was in a very bad mood.

"Hey, Kev," Walter said brightly. "What's going on?"

"What do you care," Kevin snapped.

Walter cringed. "Excuuuuse me. What's bothering you?"

"My mom," Kevin muttered. "She won't get me the sneakers I want. I'll never have enough money to buy them."

"I saw a notice on the billboard at the market that Old

Man McKenna is looking for someone to do yard work," Walter suggested.

Kevin shuddered, "No way! Brandon lives just a couple of houses down from the McKenna place, and he says that the old guy's a warlock. He heard spooky stuff like chanting coming from that place. And one time Brandon saw the old man burying something in his backyard."

Walter laughed. "Maybe his cat died. And the chanting was probably coming from his TV. Sometimes old people turn the volume up really loud because they can't hear."

Kevin frowned as he watched Franco Roberts saunter by. "Maybe you're right," he said. "I do need the money."

• • • • • • • • • •

On his way home Kevin passed Thompson's Shoe Store. In the window was an orange sign that screamed "SALE—1/2 OFF." Arranged around the sign were several pairs of shoes, including a pair of Fabulous Flyers. Another small sign urged, "Try our layaway plan."

Moments later, Kevin was turning down Raven Avenue, where Old Man McKenna lived. The house at the end of the block was shadowed by large, leafy trees, and the window shades were all pulled down. The place looked so empty that anyone would have thought it was deserted.

Hesitantly, Kevin stepped onto the porch. He reached up to ring the bell, then pulled back his hand. A plump, brown spider had anchored one corner of its web on the button. "Gross!" Kevin yelped. Then, suddenly, the door creaked open just a crack.

"What do you want?" asked a raspy voice.

"I'm Kevin Pope," Kevin stuttered, straining to see inside. "I'm here about your ad for someone to do yard work."

The door opened wider and Kevin jumped back. There stood Old Man McKenna with his wrinkled, bald head and beady, black eyes. The sneakers, Kevin reminded himself—I have to do this for the Fabulous Flyers.

"Rake the leaves," the grizzled old man said.

"I beg your pardon?" Kevin asked.

"Leaves!" he barked. "I want you to rake the leaves in the front yard!" He pointed a bony finger to a corner of the porch where a worn rake leaned against the wall. "I'll give you ten dollars to do it right now. Take it or leave it."

· · · · · · · · · ·

Within an hour Kevin had finished the job.

"I'm all done," he announced to Mr. McKenna. "Can I get my money now?"

The old man simply turned and walked down the hallway, motioning for Kevin to follow. Gathering up his courage, Kevin stepped inside the dark, dingy house. Mr. McKenna led him to a room where there were stacks of dusty old books. Bottles of strange colored fluids and powders lined every shelf.

"Wait here, and don't touch anything," Mr. McKenna ordered, then shuffled into the next room.

Kevin glanced around uneasily. He had a creepy feeling

that he wasn't alone. Then, out of the corner of his eye, he saw something move behind a pile of books, but when he looked, there was nothing there. He peered into the shadows. That was when an elaborately carved box caught his eye. It was on a low shelf, nearly hidden behind a thick book. Unlike everything else in the room, it was shiny and free of dust. Although Old Man McKenna had warned him not to touch anything, Kevin was drawn to that box.

"How's he going to know?" he mumbled, opening the lid. Much to his surprise, neatly folded in the red velvet lining was a crisp hundred dollar bill. Kevin gaped at the money, then the sound of the old man's footsteps caused him to make a decision. He plucked the bill from the box and slipped the money into his pocket. Seconds later, Old Man McKenna entered. He stood right in front of Kevin and stared into his eyes, as if he were probing the boy's thoughts. Kevin felt queasy as the man's dark eyes flashed angrily.

"Here," he grunted, holding out his hand. "One must always pay one's debts."

Kevin started to tremble. He looked down and saw the wrinkled ten dollar bill in the equally wrinkled hand.

"Thanks," said Kevin, snatching the money as quickly as he could, while trying not to touch the creepy hand. Then he backed down the hall. "I'll, uh . . . I'll stop by again to see if you need anything else done."

"Oh, I'm quite sure I'll be seeing you," the old man said without a smile.

Kevin charged through the door and ran down the street. Even without looking he was aware that Mr. McKenna was watching him from the upstairs window.

Heading straight for the shoe store, Kevin asked himself out loud, "What does an old man like that need all this money for?" But the question didn't linger long. Soon he was walking out of the store wearing a brand new pair of Fabulous Flyers, almost proud of his theft.

When he got home, Kevin was glad that his mother wasn't there. He wouldn't be able to wear the shoes openly—at least not for a while. He wrapped the sneakers in a plastic bag and stashed them in a little-used cupboard in the garage. It would be easy to retrieve them in the morning and he could change on his way to school.

• • • • • • • • • •

The following day Kevin couldn't wait to show off his prize.

"How'd you do it?" Walter asked. "You couldn't have done *that* much yard work!"

"There are ways," Kevin hedged. "Besides, what does it matter as long as I got what I wanted?"

"Well, look who's got some Flyers!" someone said.

Kevin looked up to see Nick Maston. He was the most popular kid in class. "We're getting together to shoot a few hoops after school." Nick grinned. "Want to play?"

"Sounds good," Kevin replied happily. "I'll be there."

• • • • • • • • • •

By the time the game was over, Kevin was feeling great. In his new Fabulous Flyers he had played like a champ. He had never jumped so high or turned so quickly. It almost felt as if the shoes had a life of their own. He replayed the game over and over in his mind, shot by shot, on the way home.

Then, all at once, he stopped. He was not headed home. He was standing under a sign that read Raven Avenue.

"What am I doing here?" he said in surprise. He started to walk away, but his feet seemed to turn against his will. Unable to control his own movement, he stepped into the street just as a car was speeding by. Kevin screamed, and the tires squealed as the driver slammed on the brakes and swerved.

"Idiot!" the driver yelled, as he drove off.

But Kevin couldn't stop. Step by step, he moved closer to the eerie house at the end of the block. He tried to turn back, but it was no use. Something else was directing his footsteps. As if trapped in a nightmare and powerless to end it, he was forced toward Old Man McKenna's.

As Kevin reached the path leading to the house, the front door began to open. Kevin tried to scream, but no sound came out. Somehow, he had become a prisoner in his own body. He stepped onto the sagging porch, and the door yawned wider like a gaping mouth waiting to swallow him.

The entryway was hot and stuffy. As Kevin's eyes adjusted to the darkness, he saw that someone was waiting for him. At the end of the hallway, Old Man McKenna stood glaring at him. He looked different now. Thick ringlets of white hair writhed around his shoulders like serpents. He raised his arms and held them open toward Kevin. His long, bony fingers were tipped with sharp, curved nails. Small, shadowy creatures raced back and forth at the old man's feet, chattering in high-pitched squeals.

Breathless with fear, Kevin continued to move forward against his will, step by step. He felt the shoes tighten painfully on his feet. One of the shadowy beasts raced toward him. It stopped and started in a series of jerky movements until finally it was crouched at his feet hissing up at him. Then it bared a row of tiny, needlelike teeth and lunged forward, sinking its fangs into Kevin's ankle.

"Be patient, my little ones!" the old man commanded. "I know you are hungry. It won't be much longer and we will all feed." He smiled at Kevin showing his own sharp teeth. "I hope you have enjoyed your new shoes. They have a special feature, courtesy of your own greed. You see, you acquired them with what you stole from me, so they are actually mine . . . and so is anything that is in them."

With every ounce of strength he had left, Kevin willed himself to scream, "NOOOOO!!!" He crumpled to the ground and tore at the laces of the sneakers, but they kept retying themselves. Hysterically, Kevin twisted his body and ripped the laces with his teeth. Scraping bits of skin from his ankles, he ripped the evil shoes from his feet. Barefoot and bleeding, Kevin fled down the hallway as the door began to creak closed. He managed to leap through the gap just before it slammed shut. Hot tears streamed down his face, and his ankles throbbed as he ran through the empty streets.

• • • • • • • • • •

By the time his mom arrived home, Kevin had scrubbed his battered feet and was already in bed.

"Are you okay, sweetie?" she said, sitting on the edge of the bed and feeling his forehead.

"Yeah, I'm okay," he lied. "I'm just tired." He couldn't tell her. He couldn't tell anyone . . . ever!

After his mother had left the room, Kevin lay awake for a long time, shivering. All he could think about were Old Man McKenna's horrid monsters and the sound of their sharp teeth gnashing hungrily. But he had escaped. He was safe, and he would never go near that house again! Finally, he fell into a light sleep. Then something jerked him back.

He sat up, wide awake. His darkened room was completely empty and silent, but he felt a terrible sense of dread. Then he noticed that his feet still hurt, as though something were squeezing them. He reached down to rub his sore ankles and felt something warm and smooth.

"What the—" he gasped, yanking back his hand. Even in the darkness he could see the blanket move slightly. Slowly, barely breathing, he stretched out his trembling hand and clutched at a corner of the covers. Then, in one move, he tore them away. His heart leaped to his throat. The Fabulous Flyers were on his feet! He watched with mounting terror as the laces twined around each other, tying themselves firmly, one after another, into horrible, inescapable knots.